FROST

Alpha Male Protector Romance and Suspense

A Guardian Hostage Rescue Specialists SHORT READ

ELLIE MASTERS
MASTER OF ROMANTIC SUSPENSE

JEM Publishing

Dedication

This book is dedicated to my one and only—my amazing and wonderful husband.

Without your care and support, my writing would not have made it this far.

You pushed me when I needed to be pushed.

You supported me when I felt discouraged.

You believed in me when I didn't believe in myself.

If it weren't for you, this book never would have come to life.

Also by Ellie Masters

The LIGHTER SIDE

Ellie Masters is the lighter side of the Jet & Ellie Masters writing duo! You will find Contemporary Romance, Military Romance, Romantic Suspense, Billionaire Romance, and Rock Star Romance in Ellie's Works.

YOU CAN FIND ELLIE'S BOOKS HERE:

ELLIEMASTERS.COM/BOOKS

Shop Ellie Masters Romantic Suspense and Steamy Contemporary Romance by series.

Angel Fire Rock Romance

Guardian HRS: Alpha Team

Guardian HRS: Bravo Team

Guardian HRS: Charlie Team

Guardian HRS: Delta Team

Cerberus Personal Security

The LaRouge Triplets

The One I Want Series

Angel's Peak Series

Billionaire Boy's Club

The Lovers

Changing Roles

SUGGESTED READING ORDER

START HERE

Rockstar Romance

The Angel Fire Rock Romance Series

EACH BOOK IN THIS SERIES CAN BE READ AS A STANDALONE AND IS ABOUT A DIFFERENT COUPLE WITH AN HEA.

IT IS RECOMMENDED THEY ARE READ IN ORDER.

Heart's Insanity

Ashes to New

Heart's Desire

Heart's Collide

Hearts Divided

Hearts Entwined

Forest's FALL

Hearts The Last Beat

CONTINUE HERE...

Military Romance

Guardian Hostage Rescue Specialists

Rescuing Melissa

(Get a FREE copy of Rescuing Melissa

when you join Ellie's Newsletter)

Alpha Team

Rescuing Zoe

Rescuing Moira

Rescuing Eve

Rescuing Lily

Rescuing Jinx

Rescuing Maria

Bravo Team

Rescuing Angie

Rescuing Isabelle

Rescuing Carmen

Rescuing Rosalie

Rescuing Kaye

Cara's Protector

Rescuing Barbi

Charlie Team

Rescuing Rebel

Rescuing Stitch

Rescuing Mia

Jenna's Protector

Rescuing Sophia

Rescuing Malia

Rescuing Ally (Part 1)

Rescuing Ally (Part 2)

Delta Team

Rescuing Ember

Rescuing Aria

STANDALONES IN THE GUARDIAN HOSTAGE RESCUE SERIES YOU CAN READ ANYTIME

Military Romance

Guardian Personal Protection Specialists

Sybil's Protector

Lyra's Protector

Angel's Peak Series

Steamy Instalove Small Town

Snowed in with the Mountain Doctor

Rescued by the Mountain Guide

Stranded with the Resort Owner

Matched with the Small-Town Chef

Trapped with the Forest Ranger

Snowbound with the Vineyard Owner

Reunited with the Hometown Hero

Colliding with the Coffee Shop Owner

Falling for the Firefighter

Wrecked with the Reclusive Author

Tangled with the Single Dad

Whirlwinded by the Helicopter Pilot

Sheltered by the Veterinarian

Bound by the Sheriff

The One I Want Series

(Small Town, Military Heroes)

By Jet & Ellie Masters

Saving Abby

Saving Ariel

Saving Brie

Saving Cate

Saving Dani

Saving Jen

The LaRouge Triplets

Asher

Command Me

Control Me

Collar Me

Embracing FATE

Seizing FATE

Accepting FATE

HOT READS

A STANDALONE NOVEL.

Down the Rabbit Hole

Light BDSM Romance

The Ties that Bind

EACH BOOK IN THIS SERIES CAN BE READ AS A STANDALONE AND IS ABOUT A DIFFERENT COUPLE WITH AN HEA.

Alexa

Penny

Michelle

Ivy

HOT READS

Becoming His Series

THIS SERIES MUST BE READ IN ORDER.

The Ballet

Learning to Breathe

Becoming His

Dark Captive Romance

A STANDALONE NOVEL.

She's MINE

To My Readers

This book is a work of fiction. It does not exist in the real world and should not be construed as reality. As in most romantic fiction, I've taken liberties. I've compressed the romance into a sliver of time. I've allowed these characters to develop strong bonds of trust over a matter of days.

This does not happen in real life where you, my amazing readers, live. Take more time in your romance and learn who you're giving a piece of your heart to. I urge you to move with caution. Always protect yourself.

ONE

FROST

I'M LISTENING TO TWO CARTEL MEMBERS TALK ABOUT A WOMAN'S abduction, and my hand is wrapped so tight around the glass I'm surprised it doesn't shatter.

The whiskey burns, but not nearly enough.

I should leave. Should finish this drink, pay my tab, drive back to the safe house, and sleep off three days of mandatory leave. CJ's orders were clear: *Stand down. Decompress. Get your head straight before you get yourself killed.*

"*¿Cuándo hacemos la recogida?*" When do we do the pickup?

The dive bar in Nogales is dark, loud, and exactly the kind of place where men say things they shouldn't. Jukebox drowning out thinking. Cigarette smoke thick enough to hide in. The locals at the pool table don't care about the two men who walked in fifteen minutes ago with expensive watches and concealed Glocks.

But I care.

Because I've been listening to these assholes describe this woman —American, mid-twenties—like she's inventory.

Merchandise.

And every word out of their mouths makes the dog tags under my shirt feel heavier.

"Cuando firme. Ramirez nos llamará." When she signs. Ramirez will call us.

I take another sip. Force my shoulders to stay relaxed. Keep my eyes on the amber liquid like it's the most interesting thing in the world.

This is not my problem.

This is not my mission.

I'm on *leave*, for fuck's sake. Mandatory psych eval pending. One more violation and CJ doesn't just suspend me—he terminates my contract and makes sure no other contractor will touch me.

"¿Cuánto tiempo?" How long?

"Tres horas, máximo." Three hours, max.

My jaw clenches. I force it to relax.

Three hours. She has three hours before they move her to a secondary location, and I know what that means. Once they transport, she's gone. Vanished into the cartel pipeline. Mexico, then further south. Six months from now, she'll be in some compound in Colombia or Venezuela, and nobody will ever find her.

If she's even still alive in six months.

The first man laughs, low and cruel. *"Entonces Ramirez la convencerá. De una forma u otra, ella firma esta noche."* Then Ramirez will convince her. One way or another, she signs tonight.

Convince her.

My knuckles go white on the glass.

Don't think about it. Don't picture what "convince" means in cartel speak. Don't imagine some terrified woman tied to a chair while men like these—

Sofia was tied to a chair.

The thought cuts through everything else, sharp and vicious and *wrong*. I shove it down, bury it under five years of not thinking about Caracas. About following the orders that killed her.

"Ramirez ha estado esperando un buen pedazo de culo americano. Finalmente lo consigue." Ramirez has been waiting for a nice piece of American ass. He finally gets it.

"Sí. Tres horas, luego ella es suya." Yes. Three hours, then she's his.

They clink beer bottles like they're celebrating.

I stare at my whiskey.

Call it in. That's protocol. Guardian HRS has an emergency line, 24/7 response capability, and established protocols for situations exactly like this. I pull out my phone. CJ will mobilize assets, coordinate with local contractors, and run proper intel before going in.

That's the *right* thing to do.

The *professional* thing.

The thing I'm *supposed* to do.

My phone is in my pocket. Two taps away from CJ's direct line.

I don't reach for it.

Because I'm doing the math, and the math is *brutal*.

Call comes in at—I check my watch—21:47. CJ needs authorization before mobilizing Guardian HRS assets for a non-contracted rescue. That's thirty minutes minimum, probably longer. Then team spins up: operators recalled, gear loaded, tactical plan drafted.

Optimistic timeline? Six hours from my call to boots on the ground.

She has three hours before transport.

Maybe.

And that's assuming everything goes perfectly. Assuming CJ can get authorization immediately. Assuming the team mobilizes without delays. Assuming I even have cell service to make the call from wherever these assholes are headed. Because I'm definitely following them.

Too many assumptions.

Too many variables.

Too much like Caracas, where we waited for authorization that came too late.

The second man pulls out his phone and checks something. *"Ramirez dice que está llorando. Preguntando por su hermano."* Ramirez says she's crying. Asking for her brother.

Asking for her brother.

Fuck.

My hand moves before my brain catches up—pulling cash from

my wallet, dropping it on the bar. Forty dollars for a twenty-dollar tab. I slide off the stool, moving casually and unhurried like a man who's just tired of drinking alone.

The two cartel members don't even glance my way.

Outside, the desert air hits warm and dry. Stars scatter across the sky, sharp and bright. The parking lot is gravel and dust, and three vehicles: my F-250, their white panel van, and a rusted sedan that probably belongs to the bartender.

I stand there for five full seconds.

This is the moment. This is where I make the call. Where I do the *right* thing, the *smart* thing, the thing that keeps me employed and alive and not violating every protocol Guardian HRS has.

This is where I learn from Caracas instead of repeating the same mistake.

My phone is in my hand. Screen lit. CJ's contact right there.

One tap. That's all it takes.

Sofia's dog tags are warm against my chest, metal heated by body temperature and guilt. I've worn them every day for five years. Every single day, a reminder of what happens when you follow orders instead of your gut.

She died because you didn't choose her.

Her brother's words. The last thing he said to me before walking away from Sofia's funeral.

Three hours.

I think about that woman—whoever she is—tied to a chair somewhere. Crying. Asking for her brother, who probably can't save her.

I think about Sofia, tied to a chair in Caracas, while I extracted with my team because orders are orders and assets are expendable.

I think about the psych eval I'm supposed to pass. About CJ's warning that one more violation means termination. About my career, my reputation, everything I've built since leaving Delta Force.

Then I think about living with myself if I walk away.

If I make the call, follow protocol, and she's dead before Guardian HRS can mobilize.

If I choose *right* over *fast,* and it costs another woman her life, I won't be able to live with myself.

The math is brutal and simple: She has three hours. Guardian HRS needs more.

My thumb hovers over CJ's contact.

"Fuck," I breathe into the empty parking lot.

Then I pocket my phone and walk to my truck.

Not calling it in.

Not waiting for authorization.

Not following protocol.

Going rogue. Again. Except this time I'm breaking orders instead of following them.

This time, maybe someone lives.

The cartel members emerge from the bar, still laughing, climbing into their panel van.

I wait thirty seconds.

If this costs me my career, my reputation, everything—

At least I won't have to add another set of dog tags to the one I'm already wearing.

I slide into my F-250, but don't start the engine yet. Just watch as they pull out onto Highway 82, heading east into the desert.

Then I follow.

Headlights off for the first mile, navigating by moonlight, keeping them just visible ahead. Then I flip the lights on to avoid suspicion, drop back two hundred yards. Professional tail. Not my first time tracking someone who doesn't want to be followed.

The highway cuts through open desert, sagebrush, and sand that stretches endlessly on both sides. Minimal traffic this time of night —just me and them and the empty road.

My phone buzzes. CJ.

I glance at the screen, then back to the road. Ignore the call.

It buzzes again. Text: *You good? Check in.*

I don't respond. Can't tell him what I'm doing because then he'll order me to stand down, and I won't, and that'll make everything worse.

Fifteen minutes out of Nogales, the van's brake lights flare. They turn off the highway onto a dirt access road, dust billowing in their wake.

I kill my headlights, and follow by moonlight. The road is rough, with washboard ruts that rattle my suspension. Ahead, a warehouse complex emerges from the darkness—a single building, industrial and isolated, exactly the kind of place cartels use for business they don't want witnesses to.

The van pulls up next to a black SUV already parked outside. A third vehicle, an older sedan, sits off to the side.

I stop a quarter mile out. Kill the engine. Silence rushes in, broken only by the tick of cooling metal and the distant sound of men's voices carrying across the desert.

Time to gear up.

TWO

FROST

______

I POP MY TRUCK BED STORAGE, THE LOCKS DISENGAGING WITH A SOFT click. Inside: tactical vest, suppressed Glock, AR-15, extra mags, night vision, med kit. Everything I need. I'm always prepared, even on leave. Especially on leave, because Delta Force training doesn't shut off just because you're trying to forget.

The vest settles across my shoulders, weight distributed, nothing rattling. I check the Glock—magazine full, one in the chamber, suppressor threaded tight. AR-15 slung across my back, extra mags in the vest pouches. Tac knife secured to my thigh. Night vision mounted on my helmet.

I leave my phone in the truck. Can't risk it buzzing during breach.

Then I move.

Quarter mile on foot across open desert, staying low, using scrub brush and shadow for cover. The sand is soft under my boots, muffling my steps. The warehouse grows larger with each careful advance, and I can make out details now—corrugated metal walls, windows lit from inside, three vehicles parked near the entrance.

I pull down my night vision, scan the perimeter. Two tangos outside smoking, their heat signatures bright green against the cool desert. The two men from the bar. They're facing the vehicles, backs to the open desert, talking and laughing. Sloppy.

I switch to thermal, scan through the windows. Three more signatures inside. One isolated in what looks like a back room.

Five tangos total. One potential hostage.

I've fought worse odds in worse places.

I circle wide, approaching from the building's blind side where the exterior lights don't reach. The two cartel members are still outside, now arguing about a penalty call in last week's game, completely oblivious to the fact that someone's closing in.

Both carry Glocks, safeties off, rounds chambered. Sloppy and stupid, but it tells me they're not expecting trouble out here.

Twenty feet. The smell of their cigarette smoke reaches me.

Ten feet. I can hear every word they're saying now.

Five feet. Close enough to see the Glocks poorly concealed at the small of their backs.

I move.

First tango doesn't see me until the suppressor touches his temple—too late, already dead—I'm catching his weight before his legs remember to give out.

Second tango turns, mouth opening for a shout that never comes. Double-tap. Center mass. He folds like paper.

I drag both bodies into the shadows. Thirty seconds elapsed.

The side door is unlocked. Overconfident. I test the handle slowly, feel it give, ease it open just enough to slip through.

Inside, the air is cooler, heavy with the smell of concrete dust and motor oil. Fluorescent lights hum overhead, casting harsh shadows. I move down the hallway, weapon up, each step deliberate and silent.

First tango at the front door, guard position, but he's watching the vehicles outside instead of covering his six.

Fatal mistake.

I clear the corner, line up the shot. Suppressed round to the back of the head. He drops without a sound, and I'm already moving past him.

Second room—office setup, metal desk, paperwork scattered.

Tango sitting with his back to the door, counting money in neat stacks. He never hears me. Double-tap to the back of the skull. Bills flutter as he slumps forward.

The third tango is in what passes for a break room, making coffee at a single-burner hotplate. The smell of burnt coffee fills the small space. I'm on him before he can turn, single shot, and he goes down beside the hotplate.

Five tangos down. Clean. Silent. Efficient.

I clear the rest of the warehouse methodically—storage areas filled with plastic-wrapped pallets, empty offices with broken chairs and old calendars on the walls. Nothing.

Back corner of the building. Closed door with light showing underneath.

I stack on the door, control my breathing, let my heart rate settle. Then I breach.

The woman is zip-tied to a metal chair in the center of the small room.

First thing I notice: blood dried on her temple from a head wound, dark and crusted. Bruises on her wrists where the zip ties cut in. But her eyes—that's what stops me. Sharp and alert, tracking my movement the instant I come through the door. Tactical assessment, not panic. Not relief. Cold calculation.

Not the eyes of a victim.

The eyes of someone who's been in combat.

Papers are spread on a metal table beside her. Legal documents. Printed forms. Numbers. Signature lines.

She doesn't scream. Doesn't beg. Just watches me for three full seconds, then speaks.

"Not that I mind the rescue, but who the hell are you? You bring any back up or just that scowl?" Southern accent, clear and controlled. Arresting.

I blink. Not the response I expected from someone who's been held captive for three days.

I move to her, pulling my knife from the thigh sheath. She holds completely still as I cut the zip ties, doesn't flinch when the blade comes within inches of her skin. The plastic falls away, and she immediately brings her hands up, flexing her fingers, checking circulation.

I sheath the knife, reach for her face to check her pupils. She lets me, but I can feel the tension in her, the coiled readiness to fight if I cross a line.

"How many fingers?" I hold up three.

"Three. I'm fine."

"You're bleeding."

"It's dried. I'm a medic. I know triage." She stands without my help, tests her weight on both legs. Steady. No tremor. "You military? Delta?"

No Delta operator advertises it—ever. The word's a ghost, unspoken even in whispers. "Guardian," I say instead, letting her puzzle it out. I look at her. "Can you walk?"

She meets my eyes, and there's steel there. "I can walk. But I'm not leaving."

Of course not. Nothing about this woman is easy.

"You are leaving. Now."

"Not without my brother."

I keep my voice level and controlled. "Intel said one hostage."

"Your intel was wrong." Her jaw sets, stubborn. "They took us from my apartment in Tucson three days ago. They've been keeping us separated. They're holding him somewhere until I sign." She gestures to the papers on the table.

I swept this entire building. Every room. Every closet. "Your brother's not here."

First crack in her composure—a flicker of fear in her eyes before she shoves it down. "Then they moved him. But he's alive. They said if I signed, they'd bring him back. They said they need information about what our mother left us. Some kind of—I don't know, hidden accounts or property or something. They've been interrogating him."

I look at the papers for the first time, really look. Trust fund documents. Four hundred thousand dollars. Established by Margaret Brooks. Two signature lines at the bottom: Magnolia

Brooks and Tyler Brooks. Both blank. Both required to access the funds.

Something's wrong here. The pieces don't fit.

"What's your name?"

"Maggie."

I glance at the document, at the cursive script. "Magnolia Brooks?"

Her jaw tightens, muscles flexing. "Nobody calls me that."

"Copy that."

I study the paperwork, the unsigned lines, the amount. Both signatures are required. They need her to sign. Which means whatever story her brother told her about their mother hiding something—

Outside, I hear it. Vehicles approaching fast, engines roaring, tires on gravel.

Backup. Already.

"We're out of time." I grab her arm. "Move. Now."

She pulls away from my grip, snatches the trust documents from the table. "I need these!"

I don't argue. Don't have time. She'll need to see them later anyway when she realizes what they really mean.

We move through the warehouse fast. I take point, weapon up, scanning corners. Maggie follows closely, and moves right—reading my hand signals without instruction, staying in my blind spot, keeping low. Definitely trained.

Outside, the desert air hits us warm and dry. My truck is four hundred yards away across open ground. The headlights in the distance are closing fast.

"Run."

We sprint. Sand and scrub blur past. Maggie keeps pace with me, breathing hard but controlled, no complaints, no slowing down. Behind us, the roar of engines gets louder, and then gunfire erupts— poorly aimed, panic fire, rounds kicking up dirt ten feet to our left.

We reach my truck, I get her into the passenger seat, slam the door, and slide across the hood to the driver's seat. The engine roars to life. I slam it into drive just as the first cartel vehicle comes around the warehouse.

More gunfire. Rounds ping off my armored truck bed, spider-web my rear window.

I return fire through my window, three-round burst controlled and precise. The lead vehicle's windshield shatters, and the SUV swerves hard before the driver recovers.

I floor it, and we fishtail in the sand before the tires catch. Desert dust billows behind us, and bullets are still flying, but we're pulling away, faster—my truck is built for this kind of shit.

Highway 82 stretches out ahead, a ribbon of cracked asphalt cutting through the scrub. I check the mirrors constantly: two vehicles on our tail, black SUVs kicking up their own clouds, closing the gap despite my lead. I've got the faster rig and more ground clearance, but they're persistent fucks, spraying rounds that ping off the tailgate.

Maggie doesn't freeze. Adrenaline's still pumping through her; I see it in the set of her jaw. She twists in the passenger seat, snatching the AR-15 from the rack behind us—my spare, always loaded for bear.

"Hold steady," she snaps, bracing one elbow on the windowsill as she leans out, wind whipping her hair like a storm.

The first burst from her rifle cracks sharp over the engine roar, stitching holes across the lead SUV's windshield. The driver swerves, tires spitting out rock and sand, but she adjusts, cool as ice, and fires again. The vehicle fishtails hard, flips once in a plume of dust and glass, rolling to a stop in a crumpled heap off the shoulder.

The second SUV veers to avoid it, buying her a clean shot. She nails the grille—radiator explodes in a hiss of steam—and follows with a headshot through the side window. The rig slows, veering into the ditch, no more pursuit.

Damn. I've run with some of the best—SEALs, Rangers, you name it—but that was surgical. No hesitation, no spray-and-pray bullshit. She's a force, this woman, turning the tide like it was nothing.

And now, sliding back into her seat like she just finished a range drill, she holsters the rifle and asks, casual as a Sunday drive, "Where are you taking me?"

Not a blink, not a tremor in her voice. If anything, the firefight sharpened her edges. Impressed doesn't cover it; the woman's unbreakable.

We're clear. No more bullets, just the hum of the highway and the fading echo of gunfire. She settles back, fingers tightening on those trust documents, but her shoulders betray her now—a faint quiver running through them like a low current.

Her breaths come quicker, shallower, hitching in her chest as if the air's grown too thick to pull in deep. Blood from her temple wound drips steadily, dark spots blooming on the white paper in her lap like ink from a broken pen.

"Somewhere safe."

"What about Tyler?" Her voice rises. "You have to go back for him."

I glance at the papers in her lap, at the signature lines, at the amount. Four hundred thousand dollars. Both signatures are required. Three hours until pickup after she signs. Ramirez is waiting for his prize.

The pieces are clicking together in my head, forming a picture she's not going to want to see.

Tyler Brooks isn't being held in a separate location, getting interrogated.

Tyler Brooks is making a deal.

But I can't tell her that. Not yet. Not without proof. Not while she's in shock and bleeding and still believing her brother is a victim like her.

"Priority is keeping you alive." I keep my voice flat, tactical. "Then we figure out your brother."

She stares at the blood-stained papers in her hands, and I can see her trying to make sense of it all, trying to force the pieces to fit the story she needs to be true.

I drive into the darkness, checking mirrors every few seconds, already planning our next move.

She thinks she's holding evidence that will save her brother.

She doesn't know she's holding proof he sold her.

THREE

MAGGIE

I'M WATCHING HIM DRIVE LIKE I'M CATALOGING THREATS ON A battlefield.

Military bearing—that much is evident from the way he holds himself, spine straight even when relaxed, eyes constantly scanning the mirrors with the kind of discipline that comes from training beaten so deep it's reflexive.

His hands on the wheel are steady, scarred across the knuckles, and there's a tattoo peeking out from under his right sleeve that looks like coordinates.

"Guardian," he said when I asked if he was Delta.

Not an answer, exactly—just a word, dropped like a challenge. I've heard of Guardian HRS in passing, some shadowy private outfit that handles the kind of jobs governments don't touch.

Mercenaries? Contractors? Ex-special forces playing hero for hire? Delta doesn't just go private sector without a reason. Either retired or burned out, and this man can't be more than mid-thirties. Too young for retirement. Which means something broke him badly enough that he left.

I glance at him sidelong, testing the waters. "Guardian. That's... private sector?"

The truck's interior smells like gun oil and desert dust, and my head is throbbing where they pistol-whipped me three days ago. The blood on my temple has dried crusty and tight, pulling when I move my face. I should clean it. Should assess for concussion—my pupils were equal and reactive when he checked them, but that doesn't mean I'm clear.

But I can't stop watching him, can't stop trying to figure out who this man is and why he came alone.

"Who are you?" The question comes out harder than I intend, but I'm done with people lying to me.

"Frost."

"That's a callsign, not a name."

His jaw ticks. The smallest movement, but I catch it. "You served."

It's not a question. Statement of fact, delivered flat.

"Army. Combat medic. Four years, two deployments. Afghanistan and Iraq." I shift in the seat, and the trust documents crinkle in my lap, blood-stained and wrinkled. "You?"

Long pause. The desert highway stretches empty ahead of us, nothing but darkness and the white line disappearing under the hood.

My assessment shifts, pieces clicking into place. "You're former military. I've worked out that much. Special ops or Delta, I'm guessing."

He doesn't respond, but his knuckles tighten fractionally on the wheel.

"So how did you find me?" I press. "Who sent you?"

His jaw works like he's deciding how much truth to give me. "Overheard some people talking. Followed them."

I process that for three full seconds. "You overheard? You're telling me you just happened to overhear where I was being held and decided to mount a one-man rescue operation?"

"Something like that."

"Something like—" I lean forward, ignoring the way it makes my head pound. "Where's your team?"

Silence. Just the hum of the engine and the road noise.

"Where is your team?"

"I don't have one." He says it like he's reporting the weather. "Not on this."

The implications hit me all at once. "You went rogue. For someone you've never met. Why?"

"Because you had three hours before they moved you. Guardian HRS couldn't spin up that fast."

At least that confirms one thing. He's an operative for Guardian HRS.

"Three hours?" My voice rises despite my attempt to control it. "How do you know I had three hours?"

"Because I heard them say it." He glances at me, and there's something in his eyes I can't quite read. Something that looks almost like guilt. "In a bar in Nogales. Two cartel members talking about a pickup. Three hours. After you signed whatever they needed you to sign."

I stare at him, trying to make sense of this. "So you just... followed them. With no backup. No authorization. No idea who I was or what you were walking into."

"Yeah."

"That's insane."

"Probably."

"You could have been killed."

"Wouldn't be the first time I took that risk."

Something in the way he says it makes me look closer. There's a weight to those words, a history I'm not privy to. And under his shirt, I can see the edge of dog tags—but they don't sit quite right. Like they're not his.

"You saved my life," I say finally.

"That's the job."

"It's not your job."

He doesn't respond, just keeps driving, keeps checking mirrors like he expects pursuit any second. And maybe he does. Maybe I should, too.

My fingers find the trust documents in my lap, trace the bloodstains. Tyler's name right next to mine. Both signatures required.

Four hundred thousand dollars that our mother left us, that we agreed to never touch except in emergencies.

Tyler said the cartel thinks Mother left us something valuable. Said they were torturing him for information about where it is.

But if that were true, why would they need my signature on a trust fund we both already know about?

The pieces don't fit, and that wrongness sits in my stomach like swallowed glass.

We drive for another twenty minutes before Frost turns off the highway onto a dirt road I almost miss in the darkness. The truck bounces over ruts and rocks, and every jolt sends fresh pain through my skull. I bite down on the inside of my cheek to keep from making a sound.

Ahead, a structure materializes from the darkness—a low-slung ranch house, single story, windows dark. There's a barn off to one side, half-collapsed, and a rusted water tower that probably hasn't held water in decades.

"This is your safe house?" I ask as he pulls up to the front.

"It's a safe place." He kills the engine, and the silence rushes in. "Not official Guardian HRS. Just a fallback location."

I study the building through the windshield. Single road in, which means single road out. Defensible from inside, but vulnerable if someone corners us here. "If the cartel finds us here..."

"They won't." He opens his door, and the interior light makes me squint. "Stay here while I clear it."

"I can—"

"Stay." It's not a request.

I watch him approach the house, weapon up, moving with that same fluid efficiency he showed in the warehouse. He disappears inside, and I count the seconds. Ninety-three before he reappears in the doorway and waves me in.

The interior smells like dust and disuse and something else— gun oil, maybe, or old leather. There's minimal furniture: a couch that's seen better decades, a wooden table with two chairs, and a kitchenette with a camping stove. But in the corner, there's a weapons locker that looks new, and medical supplies are spread on the table in organized rows.

"This isn't just a fallback location," I say, scanning the setup. "Someone maintains this place."

"Used to be an old Guardian HRS cache point. Decommissioned five years ago." He moves to the weapons locker and checks the contents, as if taking inventory. "But some of us keep it stocked."

"In case you needed to go rogue again?"

His shoulders tense. "In case we needed options."

I set the trust documents on the table, and they land with a soft whisper that sounds too loud in the quiet. My head is throbbing worse now, and I can feel dried blood cracking when I move my face.

Frost tosses something, and I catch it one-handed. Medical kit, military-issue, the kind I used to carry on patrol.

"Clean that head wound."

"I know how to treat a head wound."

"I know. You told me you're a medic." He says it without looking at me, still checking weapons, but there's something in his tone. Like he actually listened. Like he remembers.

I carry the kit to the cracked mirror hanging near the kitchenette and assess the damage. The cut on my temple is about two inches long, not deep enough for stitches but deep enough that it bled impressively. The blood has dried in a dark trail down the side of my face, matting my hair. There's bruising around it—the butt of a pistol, delivered with enough force to knock me unconscious when they first grabbed me.

I clean it with antiseptic, and the sting is sharp and clarifying. This I understand. Wounds have protocols. Treatment plans. Clear steps from injury to healing.

Unlike everything else that's happened in the last three days.

"You were Army," Frost says from behind me, and I can see him in the mirror's reflection, watching me work. "Combat medic. Two deployments."

"Afghanistan first. Kandahar Province. Then Iraq. Mosul." I

apply butterfly bandages, pulling the edges of the cut together. "Four years total. Got out when my contract was up."

"Why'd you get out?"

I meet his eyes in the mirror. "Why'd you leave Delta?"

"Never said I was Delta." His expression goes carefully blank.

"Didn't have to. I've worked with enough of them to know."

I turn away from the mirror and pack up the medical kit. My hands are steady, even though everything inside me is shaking. Three days of being tied to a chair. Three days of Tyler's story about the cartel thinking Mother left something valuable. Three days of believing we were both victims.

But now—

Now I can't stop thinking about the trust documents. About both signatures required. About the way those cartel members talked about a pickup after I signed.

"The trust fund." I move to the table and spread the blood-stained papers out. "This is our inheritance from our mother. She died ten years ago. Breast cancer."

Frost comes to stand across from me, his presence solid and somehow steadying. He doesn't touch the papers, just looks.

"Four hundred thousand dollars." My finger traces the amount. "Life insurance and the sale of the family property in Georgia. She set up the trust so Tyler and I would have security."

"Both signatures required." He points to the bottom of the document without touching it.

"Yes. We agreed years ago to keep it untouched. Emergency fund only." I look up at him, needing him to understand. "Our mother wanted us to have something she never had. Stability. Safety. We weren't supposed to touch it unless we absolutely needed it."

"When did the trust become accessible?"

"When Tyler turned twenty-five. He's twenty-seven now, so it's been available for two years."

"Did he ever ask to access it?"

My stomach clenches. "A few times. Said we should invest it, or split it, or—" I stop. "I always said no. It felt wrong. Like spending it would be losing the last piece of her."

Frost is watching me with those steady eyes, and I can see him processing, analyzing, putting pieces together I'm not ready to see.

"But why would the cartel care about this?" I press my hands flat on the table. "Tyler said they think Mother left us something valuable. Something hidden. That they were interrogating him about where it is. But this trust fund isn't hidden. It's legal. Documented. We both know about it."

"What exactly did Tyler tell you?" His voice is careful now. Too careful.

I think back to two days ago—the last time they let me see Tyler. Five minutes. He had a bruise on his face, and his lip was split. He looked terrified.

"He said the cartel thinks Mother had something. Money, documents, or a property deed. Something she never told us about." The memory makes my chest tight. "He said they'd been questioning him for days. That he didn't know anything, but they didn't believe him. He said if I could just sign the trust documents, it would show cooperation. Buy us time. That we'd figure out a way to escape together."

"Did you see anyone hurt him?"

The question stops me cold. "What?"

"When you saw Tyler. Did you actually see anyone hit him? Threaten him?"

I open my mouth. Close it. Think. "No. They brought him to the room alone. He had the bruise and the split lip, but I didn't— they kept us separated. I just assumed—"

"How long has Tyler lived in Tucson?"

The subject change throws me. "Three years. Why?"

"What does he do for work?"

"Logistics coordinator for a shipping company. Why are you asking about Tyler's job?"

"Does he gamble?"

My defensiveness flares hot and immediate. "No. Tyler doesn't —what does this have to do with anything?"

"Money problems? Debt?"

"No." But even as I say it, doubt creeps in. "I mean, I don't think so. He never mentioned—"

"New car recently?" Frost's questions come faster now, precise and surgical. "Nice apartment? Always seems to have cash?"

I think about Tyler's Tesla. His downtown loft with the view. The way he always picked up the check when we got dinner, waving off my attempts to split it.

"He said he got promoted," I hear myself say. "Said the company was doing well and he was moving up."

Frost pulls out a phone—not the one I saw him use before, something different. "I need to make a call."

"To who?"

"Someone who can run background." He's already moving toward the door. "Unofficial."

"Background on what?" But I already know. My stomach knows. "Frost. What are you looking for?"

He pauses in the doorway, and the pre-dawn darkness behind him makes him a silhouette. "Confirmation. Stay inside."

Then he's gone, and I'm alone with the trust documents and the growing certainty that I'm not going to like what he finds.

I sit down hard in one of the wooden chairs. It creaks under my weight. Outside, I can hear Frost's voice, low and controlled, too quiet to make out words.

I look at the trust documents again. Really look.

Both signatures required. Both are currently blank.

The cartel needed me to sign. That's why they kept me alive. That's why they didn't just—

I shut down that thought before it can finish.

But if they needed both signatures, they'd need Tyler, too. So why was Tyler kept somewhere else? Why wasn't he in that room with me?

Unless he already agreed to sign.

Unless this whole thing wasn't about what Mother left us.

Unless it was about what Tyler owed.

No. Tyler wouldn't. He's my brother. I raised him after Mother died. I made sure he finished high school, got into college, and had a future. He wouldn't—

But the new car. The nice apartment. The cash.

"He got promoted," I whisper to the empty room, but it sounds hollow even to my own ears.

I think about the last two years. How Tyler kept suggesting we split the trust fund. How he'd bring it up casually over dinner, just floating the idea. How he'd say things like, *"Mother would want us to use it, Mags. Not just let it sit there."*

How I always said no.

How he'd smile and say okay, and then bring it up again a few months later.

I think about his lifestyle. His hours. The way he'd sometimes not answer my calls for days, then show up acting normal, like no time had passed.

The way he always seemed to have money but never wanted to talk about work.

My hands are shaking. I press them flat on the table, but I can't stop the tremor.

The door opens, and Frost walks back in. One look at his face tells me everything I need to know.

"Don't," I say. "Don't tell me."

"Maggie—"

"I don't want to know."

"You need to know." He pulls up something on his phone, sets it on the table in front of me. "I had someone run Tyler's financials. Unofficial. Off the books."

The screen shows bank records. Transaction histories. Dates and amounts scrolling down in damning detail.

Sports betting. Online poker. Casino cash advances.

Wire transfers to offshore accounts.

Loans. Interest. Penalties.

Tyler's name on every single one.

"That's—" My voice cracks. "There has to be a mistake."

"Look at the dates." Frost's voice is gentle, which somehow makes it worse. "This goes back eighteen months."

I scroll through the transactions with numb fingers. Five hundred dollars here. Two thousand there. Ten thousand. Five thousand. Cash advances and loans and payments missed.

Over and over and over.

"That's not possible." But I can see the dates. Can see Tyler's account numbers. His social security number. His digital signature on loan agreements.

"Los Serpientes cartel." Frost points to a series of wire transfers. "Six months ago. First loan for eighty thousand. Couldn't pay it back. Interest compounded. Borrowed another hundred thousand to cover the first debt."

The numbers swim in front of me. "One hundred and eighty thousand dollars."

"Yeah."

"Tyler owes a cartel one hundred and eighty thousand dollars."

"Yeah."

My laugh comes out broken. "No. Tyler doesn't gamble. He doesn't—he's my baby brother. I raised him. I know him." But I can see the dates. Can see his account numbers. His social security number. His digital signature is on loan agreements.

"You knew who you thought he was." Frost pulls out the chair across from me and sits down. "People change. Especially when they're desperate."

"So what are you saying?" My voice is rising, and I can't stop it. "You're saying Tyler what—borrowed money from a cartel? Got in over his head? And then what? They just happened to kidnap both of us?"

"They didn't kidnap Tyler."

The words land like a physical blow.

"What?"

"Think about it." He leans forward, his eyes steady on mine. "Both signatures required on that trust fund. Four hundred thousand dollars. Tyler owes one-eighty. What's he got if he gets you to sign?"

"Two hundred and twenty thousand dollars." The math is automatic, mechanical. "But that doesn't—he wouldn't—"

"You weren't kidnapped because of what you know." Frost's voice is quiet and absolute. "You are *collateral* for what Tyler owes. And that trust fund? That's how he planned to pay them back. With your signature."

The room tilts. I grip the edge of the table, knuckles white.

"No." But it comes out as a whisper. "Tyler wouldn't do that. He's my brother. He—I took care of him. After my Mother died, I gave up college and went into the military so Tyler could stay in school. I made sure he had everything he needed. I—"

I'm on my feet without remembering standing. The chair scrapes against concrete, too loud in the sudden ringing in my ears. Frost is saying something, but I can't hear him through the rushing sound like static, like white noise, like my brain is trying very hard not to process what I just learned.

"Maggie—"

I shake my head. Can't. Can't do this here. Can't fall apart in front of this stranger who saved my life while my brother—while Tyler—

My stomach heaves.

I make it to the bathroom before everything comes up.

Kneeling on cracked linoleum that probably hasn't been cleaned in years, hands gripping the toilet bowl, heaving until there's nothing left. Just bile and betrayal and the taste of copper from where I bit my tongue.

Tyler sold me.

My baby brother—the one I raised after Mom died, the one I gave up college for, the one I joined the Army to support—sold me to a cartel to pay his gambling debts.

I heave again. Nothing comes up. My body trying to purge something that can't be vomited away.

Three days. I was zip-tied to that chair for three days while Tyler was—what? Negotiating terms? Counting his money? Planning how to spend the difference between four hundred thousand and one hundred eighty thousand?

Two hundred twenty thousand dollars.

That's what I'm worth to him. The profit margin on selling his sister.

My hands are shaking so badly I can't hold myself up anymore. I slide down, press my back against the bathroom wall, and pull my knees to my chest. Combat medic training notes my symptoms with detached precision: elevated heart rate, rapid shallow breathing, peripheral vision narrowing, and cold sweat.

Shock. Trauma response. Acute stress reaction.

Knowing the clinical terms doesn't make it stop.

I'm drowning in betrayal.

Six months ago.

Tyler took me to dinner at that expensive steakhouse downtown. The one with the dry-aged ribeye and the wine list that requires a second mortgage. He insisted on paying, waved off my protests with that easy grin I thought I knew.

"I got a promotion," he said, pouring us both wine from a bottle that cost more than my car payment. "Let me celebrate with my favorite sister."

I laughed. "I'm your only sister."

"Still my favorite." He lifted his glass. "To family. To Mom's memory. To having each other's backs."

We clinked glasses.

I remember thinking how proud Mom would be. How far Tyler had come. How I'd done right by her—kept him safe, kept him in school, kept him from falling apart when cancer took everything from us.

Then, casual as anything: "Hey, so I've been thinking about the trust fund. We should consider splitting it. Not all of it, just enough to invest. Mom would want us to use it, not just let it sit there."

I said no. Again. Like I always did when he brought it up.

He smiled. Kissed my cheek. Said okay.

"Whatever you think is best, Mags. You always know what's best."

Six months ago, while I sat across from him, eating expensive steak and drinking expensive wine and believing we were celebrating his success, he'd already borrowed eighty thousand dollars from Los Serpientes.

Was already gambling it away. Was already planning how to pay them back with my life.

I make a sound that's half-laugh, half-sob. It echoes off the bathroom tiles, mocking me.

The shaking gets worse. My teeth are chattering despite the desert heat. I wrap my arms around myself, trying to hold the pieces together, but I can feel them cracking apart.

Every memory is rewriting itself.

Every dinner. Every phone call. Every time he said "love you, sis" or "you're the best" or "I don't know what I'd do without you."

All of it was manipulation.

All of it was him keeping me close, keeping me trusting, so when the time came and he needed my signature on those trust documents—when he needed me terrified and desperate—I'd do exactly what he wanted.

I think about the warehouse. Three days ago. When they finally let me see him.

Tyler was brought into the room where I was tied. He had a bruise on his face. Split lip. Torn shirt.

"Maggie." His voice cracked. "God, Maggie, I'm so sorry. I'm so sorry."

I believed him.

I looked at my baby brother—hurt, scared, apologizing—and I believed every word.

"They think Mom left us something," he said. "Some hidden account or property. They've been interrogating me for days. I don't know what they want, but if we can just sign the trust documents, show cooperation, buy time—maybe we can figure out a way to escape together."

Together.

That word. That promise.

And I believed it. Because he's my brother. Because I raised him. Because family doesn't—

The sob breaks free before I can stop it. Raw and ugly and coming from somewhere so deep I didn't know it existed.

He was never kidnapped.

The bruise on his face—probably self-inflicted. Or maybe one of the cartel enforcers hit him for taking too long. For not being convincing enough.

The split lip—makeup, maybe. Or real, but not from torture. From failure.

My baby brother stood in front of me three days ago with tears in his eyes and lies in his mouth, and I fell for every single one.

I press my palms against my eyes until I see stars. But I can't unsee it. Can't unknow it.

Tyler wasn't a victim.

Tyler was the architect.

The memories keep coming, relentless and recontextualizing:

Tyler's new Tesla. "The company gave me a car allowance."

His downtown loft. "Great signing bonus with the promotion."

Always picking up the check. "Let me get this—I'm doing well."

Never wanting to talk about work details. "It's boring logistics stuff, you don't want to hear about it."

Canceling plans at the last minute. "Work emergency, sorry sis."

Not answering calls for days. "Sorry, crazy week."

Every single red flag I explained away because I trusted him.

Because he was my responsibility.

Because Mom made me promise on her deathbed: *Take care of your brother. He needs you.*

And I did. I gave up college. Joined the Army so he could stay in school. Worked overtime so he'd have spending money. Made sure he had everything Mom wanted him to have.

I loved him.

And he sold me.

The grief is physical. It's not crying—it's something rawer than that. It's my body trying to reject a reality it can't process. Shaking and heaving and making sounds I don't recognize.

I loved him.

And he sold me like I was nothing.

Like I was *inventory*.

Eventually—I don't know how long—the shaking slows. The hyperventilating eases. My combat medic brain notes the shift: acute stress transitioning to processing. Still traumatized. Still shocky. But functional.

I look up at the cracked bathroom mirror from my position on the floor.

The woman looking back is a stranger.

Blood crusted at her temple from the pistol-whip three days ago. Butterfly bandages pulling the cut closed. Face pale beneath the desert dust. Eyes red-rimmed and wild.

But not broken.

I watch her in the mirror—watch myself—and something shifts.

Tyler sold me.

That's the truth. That's the reality. That's what my baby brother—the one I raised, the one I loved, the one I would have died for—chose to do.

But I'm not dead.

I'm here. In this abandoned ranch house with a Guardian operative who went rogue to save me. I'm armed. I'm trained. I'm not that helpless woman zip-tied to a chair anymore.

Tyler made his choice.

Now I make mine.

I stand. My legs are unsteady, but they hold.

I run cold water over my hands, splash it on my face. The water is rust-brown and probably not safe to drink, but I don't care. I need to wash the vomit taste from my mouth. Need to look less like I'm falling apart.

The woman in the mirror watches me. Maggie Brooks. Magnolia Brooks. Former Army combat medic. Survivor of deployment, IEDs, and firefights.

Survivor of this, too.

I grip the edge of the sink, lean close to my reflection, and make myself say it out loud:

"Tyler sold you to a cartel. Your brother—your baby brother—gambled away everything and paid his debt with your life."

The words should break me again. Should send me back to the floor, back to the shaking and heaving.

But they don't.

Because somewhere between the vomiting and the memories and the grief—I've moved past denial.

I'm not arguing with reality anymore.

I'm not making excuses.

Tyler did this. Tyler chose this. And when those cartel members come back—because they will come back—I'm not dying for his mistakes.

Something in my chest that's been soft for twenty-seven years hardens into something sharp.

I'm walking out of this desert.

And Tyler?

Tyler is going to face what he's done.

I dry my face on my shirt. Take three more box breaths. Check my pupils in the mirror—equal and reactive, no worse than earlier. The cut on my temple is still clean, no signs of infection despite the circumstances.

I'm okay.

Not fine. Not healed. Probably won't be fine for a long time.

But okay enough to survive the next few hours.

Okay enough to fight.

I open the bathroom door.

Frost is sitting just outside, weapon in hand but lowered, positioned where he can cover both the door and the window. He doesn't ask if I'm okay—smart man, knows that's a stupid question.

Instead: "The cartel's coming. I can feel it. We need to get ready."

"Then let's get ready." My voice is steady. Steadier than I expected. "Because I'm not dying in this desert for Tyler's gambling debts."

Something shifts in Frost's expression. Not pity—respect, maybe. Understanding.

"No," he agrees. "You're not."

I move past him to the table where the weapons are laid out.

Pick up the AR-15. Check the magazine, chamber a round, and verify the safety.

Muscle memory. Familiar. Comforting.

This I understand. This I can control.

I can't control that my brother betrayed me. Can't control that I loved someone who saw me as nothing more than collateral.

But I can control this weapon. Can control my breathing, my aim, and my trigger discipline.

Can control whether I survive what comes next.

Outside, thunder rolls. The storm is getting closer.

So is the cartel.

And I'm ready for both.

FOUR

FROST

———————

I watch her shatter in real time, and there's nothing I can do to stop it.

I've seen this before. Delivered this kind of news before. Watched people's entire realities rewrite themselves when they learn someone they love isn't who they thought.

It never gets easier.

"He's the only family I have," she manages finally.

"Had." I correct her, and the past tense lands like a killing blow.

She flinches. Actual physical recoil like I hit her. Then she's pacing, to the window and back. Caged animal energy, nowhere to go, nothing to fight.

I stay seated. Give her space. Let her process.

She makes it to the wall, turns, and paces back. Her boots scuff the floor, rhythmically and harshly. "Explain it to me. All of it. How this works. How my brother—" She can't finish the sentence.

We've gone over this, but she needs to hear it again. I try to be as kind as possible, but it's an ugly truth.

"Tyler's debt goes back eighteen months," I start, keeping my voice level, clinical. Facts are easier to handle than emotions.

"Started small. Sports betting. Online poker. He was winning at first—they always let you win at first. That's how they hook you."

"Tyler doesn't gamble." But there's no conviction in it anymore.

"Tyler gambles a lot." I pull up another screen on the phone and show her. "Three different online poker sites. Sports betting across four platforms. Two casinos in Phoenix where he's a regular. The patterns are clear—he'd win some, lose more, chase the losses with bigger bets."

She's not looking at the screen. She's looking at her hands like they belong to someone else.

"Six months ago, he borrowed eighty thousand from Los Serpientes. That's not a casual loan—that's a cartel loan with cartel interest. Thirty percent compounding monthly."

"Jesus." She breathes the word.

"He couldn't pay it back. So he borrowed more. Another hundred thousand. Standard debt spiral—you borrow to cover the first loan, but now you owe both plus interest on both. It compounds fast."

"One hundred and eighty thousand." She's doing the math, and I can see her brain trying to make it make sense. "How does someone even get that deep?"

"One bad bet at a time." I've seen it before. Watched good soldiers destroy themselves the exact same way. "The cartel doesn't care how you got there. They care about collection."

"So they what—gave him two options?" She's pacing again, faster now. "Pay or die?"

"Pay or offer collateral of equivalent value."

She stops. Turns to face me. "Equivalent value to one hundred and eighty thousand dollars."

"Yeah."

"I'm not worth—" She stops herself, but I can see the calculation in her eyes. Former Army medic. American. Young. Healthy. She knows exactly what she's worth on the trafficking market, and it's a hell of a lot more than one-eighty.

"The trust fund makes it cleaner," I say before she can spiral down that path. "Tyler offers you as collateral but sweetens the deal.

Once you sign the trust documents, he withdraws the four hundred thousand. Pays the cartel their one-eighty plus interest. Walks away with the remainder."

"Two hundred and twenty thousand dollars." Her voice is hollow. "That's what I'm worth to him. The difference between four hundred thousand and his debt."

"The trust fund is the bonus." I have to tell her the rest. She needs to know it all. "You were always the primary payment."

She's shaking her head before I finish. "No. That doesn't—if they just wanted me, why would they need the trust fund at all?"

"Because Tyler's greedy. He doesn't just want to clear his debt. He wants to profit from selling you." It's a stretch. I don't know her brother, but I've seen this story too many times. My words ring true.

Her jaw tightens at the word "selling," a quick muscle twitch pulling at the corner of her mouth, like a wire snapping taut under strain. But her gaze holds steady, locked on mine, unflinching, her chin lifting just enough to carve defiance into the line of her neck.

No tears, no averted eyes—just that unyielding stare, the kind that stares down barrels and comes out swinging. This woman has steel in her spine that most operators I've served with would envy.

"So he what—staged the whole thing?" She's working through it now, following the logic. "Arranged for both of us to be taken. Told me it was about something Mother left us. Kept us separated so I couldn't see he wasn't actually being hurt."

"Yeah."

"The bruise on his face. The split lip." Her eyes go distant, remembering. "I never saw anyone hit him. He just showed up with injuries and told me they'd been interrogating him."

"He could have done those himself. Or had someone do it to make it look real."

"He looked terrified." Her voice cracks. "I thought—God, I actually thought he was trying to protect me. He said if I signed, it would buy us time. That we'd escape together."

I don't say anything. There's nothing to say that isn't just confirming what she already knows.

"So the whole kidnapping was theater." She's pacing again, but different now. Angry. "Three days tied to a chair. Three days thinking we were *both* victims. And the entire time, he was—what? Negotiating his payout?"

"Yeah." I pull up another screen. "Guardian HRS traced Tyler's movements. Four days ago, he was in Phoenix. Meeting with a cartel lieutenant at a restaurant. They have surveillance footage."

"Show me." Maggie cuts in, her voice slicing through the air like a blade. She's on her feet now, edging closer to the table, eyes fixed on me with that unblinking intensity.

"Maggie—"

"Show me."

I turn the phone so she can see, angling the screen just right under the dim overhead light, her breath catching as the footage flickers to life on the grainy black-and-white feed, timestamp ticking in the corner: 14:32, four days back.

She's transfixed, leaning in close enough that I catch the faint scent of her—sweat and resolve—as the scene unfolds: there, in the restaurant's shadowed booth, her brother Tyler pulls out his own phone with a casual flick, sliding it across the table toward the man in the expensive suit, the cartel lieutenant leaning forward with predatory interest.

The footage captures the glow from Tyler's screen illuminating their faces, sharpening Tyler's easy grin as he taps something and zooms in on the screen. Then it resolves—a pretty picture of her, Maggie, filling Tyler's display, captured in a candid shot that steals the breath: sunlight catching her smile mid-laugh, hair tousled just so, eyes bright with that unknowing trust.

Tyler points at it, nodding like he's auctioning off the prize. Then he offers his hand, making a deal.

Maggie watches it three times without speaking. Then she turns away, walks to the window, and presses her forehead against the glass. Her shoulders are shaking, but she's not making a sound.

I give her five minutes. Then I ask the questions she needs to answer.

"When was the last time you actually saw Tyler? Before this."

"Two months ago." Her voice is muffled against the glass. "He came to my apartment. Said he wanted to take me to dinner. His treat. We went to this expensive place downtown."

"Did he ask about the trust fund?"

Long pause. "Yes. Said we should invest it. Or at least split it. That Mother would want us to use it, not just let it sit there."

"What did you say?"

"I said no. Like I always do." She turns to look at me, and her eyes are red but dry. "He smiled. Said okay. That he understood, and then he picked up the check like always, and we went home."

"He was already in debt by then."

"He was already planning this." The realization settles over her like a weight. "That dinner was—what? Reconnaissance? One last try to get me to sign willingly before he moved to plan B?"

"Probably."

"And plan B was selling me to a cartel." She laughs, but it's broken and bitter. "My baby brother. The kid I raised. The one I gave up everything for."

I think about Sofia. About the choice I made in Caracas. About the five years I've spent wearing her dog tags and wondering if I could have saved her if I'd just chosen differently.

"People make choices," I say carefully. "Bad ones. Selfish ones. That's on them, not on the people they hurt."

"Is it?" She turns fully to face me now. "Because I keep thinking about all the ways I failed him. All the times I said no to splitting the trust. All the times I was too busy or too tired to notice he was drowning."

"He wasn't drowning. He was gambling."

"Maybe he was gambling because I wasn't there. Because I was too focused on being the responsible one, the adult, the—" She stops. "I don't even know anymore."

"You're not responsible for his choices."

"Then why does it feel like I am?"

I don't have an answer for that. I've been asking myself the same question about Sofia for five years.

The silence stretches between us, heavy with things neither of us wants to say. Outside, the wind picks up. Desert storm rolling in. I can smell the electricity in the air, that sharp ozone scent that comes before lightning.

"Where is he now?" Maggie asks, finally. "Tyler. Where is he?"

"My contact's still tracking that. Best guess is Phoenix. Waiting for confirmation that you signed before he collects his payout."

"Does he know I'm out?"

"The cartel would have contacted him immediately when they lost you. So yeah. He knows."

"And what does he do now?"

That's the question I've been dreading. "Either he runs, takes whatever money he has, and disappears. Or—"

"Or?"

"Or he tries to make a new deal with the cartel. You're still valuable to them."

She absorbs that without flinching.

"I think he sold you once already. I don't think he'd have moral qualms about doing it again."

"Right." She nods like that's reasonable. Like her brother hunting her for a cartel is just a logical next step. "So what do we do?"

"We?" I raise an eyebrow.

"You came for me alone. Against orders. You're in this now whether you want to be or not."

"True." The words come out before I can stop them. "Was in it the second I heard those men talking in the bar."

"Why?" She crosses her arms, studying me. "Why did you come? You don't know me. You risked your career, maybe your life, for a stranger. That's not standard operating procedure."

"No. It's not."

"So why?"

FIVE

FROST

I LOOK AT THE DOG TAGS UNDER MY SHIRT, FEEL THEIR FAMILIAR weight. "Because five years ago, I made a choice. Follow orders or save someone. I chose to follow orders. And someone died because of it."

"Caracas." She says it like she already knew. "You mentioned it in the warehouse."

"Yeah. Caracas." I run my hand over my face, feeling the stubble, the exhaustion. "CIA operation. Cartel target. We needed local assets for intel. There was a woman—Sofia. She fed us information for three months. Good intel. Made the whole operation possible."

"What happened?"

"We got our target. Extracted him. Mission successful." The words taste like ash. "But the cartel figured out Sofia helped us. Put a price on her head. I had a choice—stay and protect her, or follow my orders and leave with the team."

"You followed orders."

"Yeah. I followed orders. Sofia was killed six hours later." I touch the dog tags through my shirt. "Her brother gave me these. Said, 'She died because you didn't choose her.'"

Maggie's quiet for a long moment. "And you've been wearing them ever since."

"Every day. Reminder of what happens when you put protocol over people."

"That's why you broke protocol for me."

"Yeah." I meet her eyes. "I heard those men talking about you in that bar, and I had the same choice. Call it in, let Guardian HRS handle it through proper channels. Or go rogue and do it myself."

"You went rogue."

"I went rogue. And this time, someone lived." I lean back in the chair, feel it creak under my weight. "That's because of you, not me. You kept pace during the extraction. You stayed tactical under fire. Most civilians would have frozen or panicked. You fought."

"I'm not a civilian. Not really." She touches her temple, where the bandage covers the head wound. "Four years in-country teaches you how to move under fire."

"Yeah. I noticed." And I did. Noticed the way she read my hand signals. The way she stayed in formation without being told. The way she didn't slow me down even once. "You're good in a firefight."

"You're good at rescuing people who don't know they need rescuing."

"Usually I'm good at following orders and letting people die." The bitterness surprises me. I thought I'd buried that deeper.

She crosses the room and sits down in the chair across from me again. "You can't save everyone."

"I know."

"Sofia wasn't your fault."

"I made a choice. She died. That's cause and effect."

"You followed your superiors' orders. That's different."

"Is it?" I echo her words from earlier. "Because I keep thinking about all the ways I could have saved her if I'd just chosen differently."

"You'd probably be dead." She says it matter-of-factly. "You stay behind to protect a local asset against direct orders, you're going up against a cartel alone. Those aren't good odds."

"Better than hers."

"Maybe. Or maybe you both die, and Guardian HRS loses an operator and an asset, and the cartel wins anyway." She leans forward, her eyes intense. "You can't rewrite history by wearing dog tags and punishing yourself."

"I'm not punishing myself. I'm remembering."

"Same thing."

Maybe she's right. Probably she's right. But I've been doing this for five years, and I don't know how to stop.

A low rumble rolls through the thin walls of the old building, vibrating the warped wooden beams overhead like a warning growl from the horizon. Dust sifts down from the rafters in fine motes, caught in the stale air as another peal builds, deeper this time, shaking the rattling window panes.

Lightning flashes. Thunder rolls. The storm hits with desert fury, turning the night electric-white and shadow-black.

"Storm's coming," I say, grateful for the subject change. "Generator in this place is old. Might lose power."

"How long do we stay here?"

"Until I hear back from Guardian HRS with Tyler's location. Or until the cartel finds us. Whichever comes first."

"You think they'll find us?"

"I think they're looking. This isn't some random kidnapping crew—Los Serpientes is mid-level cartel. Professional. They don't lose assets and shrug it off."

"I'm an asset now." She says it flat. "Not a person. Not Tyler's sister. Just inventory that walked away."

"To them, yeah."

"What am I to you?"

The question catches me off guard. "What?"

"You keep talking about choices. About saving people. About making it personal." She holds my gaze, steady and unwavering. "So what am I to you? Another rescue? Another chance to choose right? Or something else?"

I should lie. Should keep it professional. Should maintain the distance that keeps operators alive and civilians safe.

But I'm so tired of lying.

"I don't know yet," I admit. "But you stopped being just another rescue the second you made that joke about my scowl."

The corner of her mouth twitches. Almost a smile. "That wasn't a joke. You do scowl a lot."

"Occupational habit."

"Along with going rogue and ignoring orders?"

"That, too."

The almost-smile fades. "What happens when your team finds out what you did? Going unauthorized. Solo op. No backup."

"CJ will have my ass." I think about the ignored calls, the unanswered texts. "Probably suspend me pending review. Maybe terminate my contract."

"Because you saved my life."

"Because I broke protocol." I run my hand through my hair. "Caracas put me on thin ice. This might break it."

"I'm sorry."

"Don't be. I made my choice. I'd make it again."

She studies me for a long moment. "You really would, wouldn't you?"

"Yeah."

"That's either really brave or really stupid."

"Probably both."

Lightning flashes outside, closer now. The thunder follows three seconds later—less than a mile away. The overhead light flickers once. Twice. Then dies.

The generator kicks in with a grinding protest, and the light comes back on, but dimmer now. Unreliable.

"Great," Maggie mutters. "Are we going to have power?"

"For a while. Generator's got fuel. But it's old. Storm might kill it completely."

"And then?"

"Then we're in the dark until morning." She drops into the opposite side of the couch, tucks her knees tight to her chest. Looking lost. Vulnerable.

And—Jesus—fucking amazing.

Even like this, curled small in the flickering light, her hair a wild tangle from the fight, smudges of dust on her cheeks, those wide eyes shadowed but sharp... she's got this raw pull, all curves and fire under the worn tank top and jeans that hug her just right, the kind of beauty that hits like a gut punch—strong lines in her jaw, full lips pressed thin, a body built for survival and something softer, warmer, if you'd let yourself imagine it.

My mind flashes there unbidden: peeling away the layers, tracing the strength in her thighs, the give of her against me. Heat stirs low, uninvited, but I shut it down hard.

Not now.

Not here.

Not when cartel shadows are closing in, her brother's betrayal is still bleeding fresh, and one wrong move could get us both killed. She's a survivor—not a distraction I can afford. I drag my gaze to the window, force it on the storm instead.

Another flash of lightning. The temperature's dropping fast—desert nights get cold quick, especially when storms blow through.

Her arms cross tight over her chest, fingers digging into the thin cotton of her t-shirt sleeves as if to anchor them, but the chill wins out—a subtle tremor starts in her shoulders, rippling down to her elbows, the fabric pulling taut with each involuntary shudder that rocks her frame against the draft seeping through the shelter's cracks.

Goosebumps prickle along her exposed collarbone where the shirt dips, and her knees draw up a fraction as she curls inward, chasing warmth that isn't there.

"There's a blanket in the back room," I say, standing. "I'll grab it."

"I'm fine."

"You're cold."

"I've been colder."

"That doesn't mean you have to stay cold now."

I find the blanket—military-issue wool, scratchy but warm—and bring it back. She takes it without argument this time, wraps it around her shoulders. The dried blood on her temple looks even darker against her pale skin.

"You should try to sleep," I tell her. "A few hours, at least. You've been through hell."

"So have you."

"I'm trained for this."

"So am I," she murmurs, the words slipping out soft and frayed at the edges, her voice barely rising above the storm's low growl outside.

But her eyelids droop heavy as she forces the sentence through, lashes fluttering like she can't quite keep them propped open, dark smudges blooming under her eyes like bruises from nights without rest.

Her head tips forward a fraction before she catches it, jaw clenching in a brief, futile fight, while her free hand drifts to her temple, pressing there as if to steady the sudden weight dragging at her after the relentless pull of three sleepless days etched in every tensed line of her body.

"Bed is yours." I gesture to it. "I'll keep watch."

"Where will you sleep?"

"I don't sleep on ops."

"Is that what this is? An op?"

The same question she asked in the warehouse, but it lands differently now. Heavier. Loaded with everything we're not saying.

"It's supposed to be," I admit.

She's quiet for a moment. Then: "But it's not. Is it?"

"No. It's not."

"When did it stop?"

I think about that. About the moment in the warehouse when she cracked that joke. About watching her keep pace during the extraction. About the way she's holding herself together even as her entire world shatters.

"Probably the second I heard those men talking about you," I say. "I just didn't know it yet."

She nods like that makes sense. Like it's not the most unprofessional thing I've ever admitted to a civilian.

The generator coughs. The light flickers again. This time it takes longer to come back on.

"We might lose power completely," I warn her.

"I'm not afraid of the dark."

"I know." I move to the window, check the perimeter out of habit, even though I can't see much through the rain now streaking the glass. "But the dark makes it harder to see threats coming."

"Do you think they'll come tonight? The cartel?"

"Depends on how good their tracking is. How motivated they are. How much losing you pisses them off." I turn back to face her. "My guess is they'll regroup, reassess, and come at us when they're ready. Not in the middle of a storm."

"But you're not sure."

"I'm never sure. That's why I keep watch."

She pulls the blanket tighter; her hands shaking. Not from cold. From everything else. From the truth about Tyler. From the fear she's trying so hard not to show.

"Come here," I say before I can think better of it.

She looks up. "What?"

"You're freezing. And shaking. And you need to conserve energy." I sit down on the couch, leaving room beside me. "Shared body heat. It's tactical."

"Tactical." She almost smiles. "That's what we're calling it?"

"Unless you have a better word."

She considers for a long moment. Then she moves over, sits beside me, careful to maintain distance even though that defeats the entire purpose.

"This doesn't work if you're three feet away," I point out.

"I'm not three feet away."

"You're close enough that I can feel the cold radiating off you."

"Maybe you're just warm."

"Maybe you're stubborn."

"Definitely stubborn." But she shifts closer.

I reach over, pull her against my side. She goes rigid for a second, then gradually relaxes, her head coming to rest on my shoulder. The blanket pools around both of us, and her trembling starts to ease.

"This is probably not standard Guardian protocol," she murmurs against my shoulder.

"There's no protocol for this."

"For what?"

"For any of this." I keep my voice low. "For going rogue. For staying. For—" I stop, but she finishes for me.

"For caring."

"Yeah. For caring."

We sit like that in the quiet, listening to the storm outside, the rain hammering the roof, the thunder rolling closer. The generator coughs and sputters but keeps running. The single overhead light flickers but holds.

"Frost?" Her voice is soft, almost hesitant.

"Yeah?"

"Thank you. For helping me. Even if it costs you everything."

I look down at her, at the blood-stained bandage on her temple, at the way she's trying so hard to hold herself together even though her brother sold her, and her entire life fell apart.

"You're worth it," I tell her, and mean it more than I've meant anything in five years.

She's quiet for a long time. Then: "I used to think family was everything. That blood meant something. That Tyler would always —" She stops. "I don't know what I think anymore."

"You think you survived. That's enough for now."

"Is it?"

"It has to be."

My phone buzzes in my pocket, and we both tense. I pull it out, check the screen.

Message from Guardian HRS. Three lines of text that make my blood run cold.

LOS SERPIENTES POSTED $50K BOUNTY ON MAGNOLIA BROOKS—ALIVE

TYLER BROOKS MEETING WITH CARTEL LIEUTENANT IN PHOENIX—2 HOURS AGO

SIX ENFORCERS DISPATCHED TO YOUR AREA—ETA UNKNOWN.

REINFORCEMENTS INBOUND.

Maggie sees my face change. "What is it?"

I show her the screen.

She reads it once. Twice. Then looks up at me. "Tyler met with them. Two hours ago."

"Yeah."

"So he's not running. He's helping them find me."

"Yeah."

She absorbs that without flinching. I'm starting to realize this woman doesn't break easily.

"Six enforcers," she says, looking at the screen again. "That's a lot for two people."

"They're not taking chances after what happened at the warehouse."

"ETA unknown. Could be hours. Could be—"

The perimeter alarm I initiated when we arrived screams through the silence, harsh and immediate.

We both freeze.

Then I'm moving, weapon up. I shift to the window. Headlights in the distance, multiple vehicles approaching fast.

"They're here," I say.

Maggie's already on her feet, blanket discarded, moving to the weapons locker. She pulls out the Glock I showed her earlier, checks it with the experience of someone who's done this a thousand times.

She looks at me, and there's no fear in her eyes. Just cold determination.

"Rules of engagement?" she asks.

I meet her gaze, and something shifts between us. Not partners. Not operator and civilian. Something else. Something I don't yet have a name for.

"We don't let them take you," I tell her. "Kill them all."

She nods once. Chambers a round. "Copy that."

I've fought worse odds.

But never with someone I'm starting to realize I can't afford to lose.

SIX

MAGGIE

The Glock feels like coming home.

I chamber a round with muscle memory so deep it's automatic, check the mag even though I watched Frost load it twenty seconds ago, test the weight in my hand. Fifteen rounds plus one in the chamber. Not enough for six trained enforcers, but it's what I have.

Product. That's what I am to my brother. To the cartel. Not Maggie Brooks, combat medic, sister, person. Just *inventory* with a fifty-thousand-dollar price tag. Or two-hundred and twenty, if you're my brother.

The thought should terrify me. Maybe it will later. Right now, it just makes me angry.

Frost is at the window, night vision down, counting. "Six tangos. Two vehicles. Heavily armed. May be more. Can't be certain. Probably no more than eight." His voice is steady, clinical. Combat mode. "They're staging at the road junction. Half a click out."

Half a kilometer. Close enough to be a problem. Far enough that we have time.

"Why are they waiting?" I move to the window beside him, staying low, weapon ready.

"Assessing the location. Planning their approach." He glances at me, and I catch something in his expression I can't quite read. "Professional. They're not rushing in like the warehouse crew."

"Because they know you're here now. They know what you can do."

"They know what we can do." The correction is subtle but deliberate. "You dropped those vehicles. They'll factor that in."

The *we* hits different than it should. Like we're a team. Like we're something other than a combat medic and a rogue operator trapped in an abandoned ranch with six killers closing in.

"How long do we have?" I ask.

"Ten minutes. Maybe fifteen." He pulls back from the window and starts checking weapons in the locker with efficient, practiced movements. "They'll send someone to scout first. Test our defenses. Once they know what they're dealing with, they'll commit."

"So we have time to prepare?"

"Some." He pulls out an AR-15, checks it, and then hands it to me along with three magazines.

I take it, check the action, sight down the barrel.

Something shifts in his expression. Respect, maybe. Or something darker. Are you scared?"

"I'm not scared." It's mostly true. The fear is there, cold and heavy in my stomach, but it's buried under something sharper. Fury. At Tyler. At the cartel. At every man who ever looked at a woman and saw dollar signs instead of a person. "I'm angry."

"Angry works." He moves to the table and starts laying out ammunition, weapons, and supplies with the precision of someone who's done this countless times. "Channel it. Use it. Don't let it make you reckless."

"I've been in firefights before. I know how to operate under pressure."

"Combat medic firefights are different than this."

"How?"

He looks at me, and there's something raw in his eyes. "Because this time you're the target. You're shooting to kill. You're not the one patching up the casualties. That changes things."

He's not wrong. Every firefight I've been in, I was behind the lines. Waiting for the wounded. Trying to put people back together after violence tore them apart. I've never been the one actively trying to kill another human being.

The distinction matters more than I want to admit.

"So what's the play?" I move to the table and start loading magazines. My hands are surprisingly steady. "They come in hard, we defend?"

"We make them pay for every inch." He's moving furniture now, creating barriers, setting up fields of fire. "Windows are our advantage. We can see them coming. Pick them off before they breach."

"And if they get inside?"

"They won't." He says it with absolute certainty, but I hear what he's not saying. If they get inside, we're done.

I help him fortify, moving the couch to block the front door, stacking the chairs to create cover near the windows. My head is throbbing where they hit me three days ago, and my wrists ache from the zip ties, but the adrenaline is pushing through it.

Combat focus, narrowing everything down to movement and tactics, and staying alive.

Outside, I hear engines. The sound is closer now. They're moving up.

Frost positions me at the east window, checks the AR-15, and hands me extra mags.

"Stay low." His gaze is locked on mine. "Pick your shots. They want you alive, which means they'll try to suppress rather than kill. That gives us an edge. Oh, and Magnolia?"

"What?" I whisper back, my breath hitching sharply.

"Aim to kill."

The words drop flat, no trace of drama, just cold fact amid the thunder's rumble—and it hits like a spark to dry tinder.

My lips twitch and quiver as I bite down hard on the inside of my cheek. A choked snort escapes before I clamp it down, and my eyes water with effort as a near-hysterical giggle claws up from the stress-knotted core inside of me.

Oblivious to my attempts not to snort, he takes the west window, and we wait.

The storm has passed, leaving the desert air clean and cold. Through the window, stars scatter across the sky, beautiful and indifferent. The kind of night that would be peaceful if six men, maybe eight, maybe more, weren't coming to drag me back to a cartel that sees me as merchandise.

Tyler helped them. While I was here in this abandoned ranch, learning the truth about what he'd done, he was in Phoenix making new deals. Helping them track me. Selling me again.

My hands tighten on the rifle.

"Maggie." Frost's voice cuts through my spiral. "Stay present. Stay focused."

"I'm focused."

"You're thinking about your brother."

"How do you—"

"Because I know that look. I've worn it." He shifts position, checking sight lines. "And thinking about him right now gets you killed."

He's right. I force Tyler out of my head, focus on the window, on the darkness outside, on the sound of engines getting closer, then stopping.

Silence.

"They're here." Frost's voice is glacial cold.

My heart is pounding, but my breathing stays controlled. Four count in. Four count out. Combat breathing. The thing they teach you in basic that actually works when everything's going to hell.

"Contact," Frost says softly. "Single tango. Fifty meters. Moving toward the barn."

I see him through my window—shadow against shadows. A scout. Testing our response.

"Do we engage?" I ask.

"Not yet. Let him get closer. Make the shot count."

The scout moves forward. Forty meters. Thirty. He's using cover well, moving from scrub brush to rock outcropping, weapon up and ready.

Twenty meters.

"Wait for it," Frost murmurs.

Fifteen meters.

The scout stops. Scans the building. I can see his night vision sweeping across the windows, and I hold perfectly still.

Ten meters.

"Now."

Frost's shot is nearly silent—a suppressed round that drops the scout like someone cut his strings. The man falls without a sound, and Frost is already shifting position.

"That tells them we're here and we're awake," he says. "They'll reassess. Commit to a full assault."

"How long?"

"Minutes." He glances at me. "You good?"

"Yeah." My hands are steady on the rifle. "I'm good."

But I'm not good. I'm watching a dead man bleed out in the dirt, and my brother helped put him there. Helped put me here. Sold me for two hundred and twenty thousand dollars and his freedom from a debt he created.

"Maggie." Frost's voice again, pulling me back. "Look at me."

I turn my head, meet his eyes in the darkness.

"You're not alone in this," he says. "Whatever happens. You're not alone."

"I've been alone since my mother died." The words come out before I can stop them. "Ten years of being the strong one. The responsible one. The one who holds everything together while everyone else falls apart."

"Not tonight. Tonight you've got me."

"One operator against six enforcers. That's not exactly good odds."

"I've fought worse." He shifts position, checks the perimeter again. "And I have you."

"Me? I don't know how much that helps things."

"You can shoot. You can move. You can think under pressure. That's more than most people I've served with."

I'm an asset. Not a product. Not inventory. An asset in the military sense—someone valuable, capable, worth protecting.

The distinction shouldn't matter, but it does.

"They're moving," Frost says, and I snap back to the window.

This isn't going to be easy.

Frost drops the second one with a headshot. The third with a double-tap to the center mass.

Those that remain scatter, taking better cover, returning suppressing fire. Rounds punch through the wall above my head, and I duck instinctively.

"You hit?" Frost's voice is sharp.

"No. I'm good." I rise, sight through the window, and squeeze the trigger. The AR-15 kicks against my shoulder, familiar and solid. My target drops—clean torso shot.

One left.

Except, I count two shadows.

"Frost…"

"I see them."

These two are smart. They've identified our positions, and they're flanking—one moves toward Frost's window, one toward mine.

"Switching positions," Frost says, already moving. "Cover me."

I lay down fire toward the tango on my side, forcing him to take cover, while Frost relocates to the north window. Better angle. Better sight lines.

His shot drops one of the shadows.

One left.

Maybe.

But this one has had enough. There's silence for what feels like an eternity. An engine roars to life and headlights swing around. He's running.

Frost's shot takes out the driver's side tire, and the vehicle lurches to the side. The last tango abandons it, disappears into the darkness.

Silence.

Six tangos down. One fled.

I'm breathing hard now, adrenaline crashing, and my hands are starting to shake.

"Stay sharp," Frost says. "Could be a feint. Could be waiting for backup."

"Or he's running back to report."

"Yeah." He moves through the ranch, checking angles, securing the perimeter. "Which gives us maybe an hour before more arrive."

"An hour." I lower the rifle, feel the tremor in my arms. "So what do we do?"

"We prepare for round two." He starts reloading magazines, the movements automatic and efficient. "And we hope Guardian HRS arrives before the cartel comes through with more enforcers."

I help him reload, my hands finding their rhythm despite the shaking. *This* I know how to do. *This* makes sense. Unlike everything else that's happened in the past three days.

"Frost?" My voice is quieter than I intend.

"Yeah?"

"In the warehouse. When you cut me loose. You looked at the trust documents, and I saw your face. You almost said something."

His hands go still on the magazine he's loading. "Yeah."

"You asked me my name, but then called me Magnolia. My full name."

"You said nobody calls you that."

"Nobody does." I set down the magazine and lean against the table. "But you looked at that document and you said it."

"Yeah. I did."

"Why?"

He's quiet for a long moment. "Because it's a beautiful name. And I don't know why you hate it so much."

The honesty catches me off guard. Most people don't ask. They just accept that I go by Maggie and move on. But Frost is looking at me like he actually wants to know.

"My mother named me after the state flower," I hear myself say. "Georgia's state flower. Magnolia. She said it was a symbol of southern beauty and strength. Grace and resilience."

"Sounds like her vision for you."

"Yeah. She had this whole picture of who I'd be. Delicate. Beautiful. The kind of daughter who'd make her proud. Who'd marry well and have babies and host dinner parties and—" I stop, feeling the familiar tightness in my chest. "Be everything she was before cancer took it all away."

Frost doesn't interrupt. Just listens with that same steady focus he brings to everything.

"She died when I was twenty. Tyler was seventeen." I'm pacing now, unable to stand still. "And suddenly I wasn't Magnolia anymore. I was the adult. The one who paid the bills and made sure Tyler finished high school and kept us from falling apart."

"So you became Maggie."

"I became whoever I needed to be. Joined the Army because we needed the money and the benefits and because someone who was delicate and beautiful couldn't do what needed doing." My voice cracks. "I spent ten years not being Magnolia. Being strong instead of beautiful. Being hard instead of graceful. Taking care of Tyler because that's what our mother would have wanted."

"And Tyler betrayed you."

The words land like a physical blow. "Yeah. He betrayed me."

"So being Magnolia didn't work, and being Maggie didn't work." Frost sets down the magazine, moves closer. "Maybe the problem isn't which name you use. Maybe the problem is trying to be what other people need instead of who you are."

"I don't even know who that is anymore."

"Yeah, you do." He's close enough now that I can see the shadows under his eyes, the stubble on his jaw, the way he's looking at me like I'm something other than a rescue or an asset or a problem to solve. "You're the woman who made a joke about my scowl while she was zip-tied to a chair. Who kept pace during extraction without slowing me down. Took out two vehicles without blinking. Who's standing here reloading magazines after a firefight like it's just another Tuesday."

"That's just training. Survival."

"That's you." His hand comes up, cups my face with surprising gentleness. His thumb traces the edge of the bandage on my temple. "Magnolia or Maggie or whoever you decide to be tomorrow. That's you surviving."

I should step back. Should maintain distance. Should remember that this is a combat situation, and we're not safe, and six cartel enforcers just tried to kill us. One got away. And there's probably more coming.

But I don't want to step back.

I want to step forward.

"Frost—"

"Colt." His voice is rough. "My name is Colt. Coulten Harrison."

"Colt." Testing it. It fits him better than Frost, somehow. Warmer. More human. "I need—"

"What do you need?"

Everything. Nothing. Something that isn't fear or anger or the hollow ache of Tyler's betrayal.

"Something real," I manage. "Everything else—Tyler, family, who I thought I was—it's all lies. But this—" I gesture between us, this strange connection forged in violence and truth. "This feels real."

"It is real."

"How do you know?"

His hand comes up, cups my face, and his eyes are so dark, they're almost black. "Because I haven't felt anything like this real in five years. Not since Caracas. Not since I stopped letting myself feel anything that mattered."

I should step back. Maintain distance. Remember we're not safe, that violence closed in once and will close in again.

But I don't want to step back.

I want to step forward. Want to grab something good before the world catches fire again.

"And I matter?"

"Yeah, Magnolia. You matter."

The name on his lips doesn't sound like an insult or a memory I'm trying to escape. It sounds like a promise.

"The cartel could come back." I move closer.

"They will." His thumb traces my lower lip.

"We could die."

"So maybe we stop wasting time." Then his mouth is on mine, and it's not soft.

Not gentle.

Desperate and angry, needing to feel something other than betrayal and loss. His hands tighten on my face, and then he's kissing me back with the same intensity, the same need.

We shouldn't be doing this. Seven men just tried to capture me. More are probably coming. We're in an abandoned ranch with limited ammunition and no backup, and a fifty-thousand-dollar bounty on my head.

But right now I don't care.

Right now, I need this to be real.

His hands slide down to my waist, pull me closer, and I go willingly. The rifle clatters against the table as I set it down, reaching for him instead. My fingers find the hem of his shirt, slide underneath to feel warm skin, hard muscle, and the raised edges of scars.

He pulls back just enough to look at me. "Magnolia—"

"Don't." I cut him off. "Don't tell me this is a bad idea. Don't tell me I'm not thinking straight. I know exactly what I'm doing."

"Do you?"

"I'm choosing something for me. Not for Tyler. Not for my mother's memory. Not because I'm supposed to or because someone needs me to." I meet his eyes. "For me. Because I want this. Because I want you."

Something shifts in his expression. "You're sure?"

"I've never been more sure of anything."

He kisses me again, and this time it's different. Not desperate. Deliberate. Like he's memorizing the taste of me, the feel of me, the way I fit against him.

My back hits the wall, and his body presses into mine, solid and warm and real. His hands are everywhere—my waist, my hips, sliding up under my shirt to trace the curve of my ribs. I arch into him, needing more, needing everything.

"Colt—" His name breaks on a gasp as his mouth finds the hollow of my throat.

"Say it again."

"Colt."

His hands tighten on my hips, pulling me harder against him. I can feel the dog tags under his shirt, pressed between us, Sofia's ghost a reminder that he's done this before—chosen feeling over protocol, chosen a person over orders.

Chosen wrong and spent five years punishing himself for it.

But right now he's choosing me.

I reach up, pull his face back to mine, and kiss him with everything I have. All the fear and anger and grief I've been holding in for three days. For ten years. For however long I've been trying to be something I'm not.

IIis shirt comes off. Then mine. Skin against skin, his hands mapping me like terrain, finding every place that makes me gasp. I'm shaking, but not from the cold.

Not from fear, but from the sheer relief of feeling something good after days of nothing but terror.

"Magnolia." He says my full name against my neck, and it doesn't sound delicate or fragile. It sounds strong. Real. Like he's seeing all of me—Magnolia and Maggie and whoever I'm becoming —and choosing it all.

"I'm not—" I start, but he stops me with another kiss.

"You're not what?"

"Delicate. Beautiful. What she wanted me to be."

"No." His hands frame my face again, forcing me to look at him. "You're better. You're strong. Capable. Brave. You survived your brother selling you and a cartel hunting you, and you're still here. Still fighting. That's not delicate. That's fierce."

The word breaks something open in my chest.

"The woman your mother wanted you to be?" Colt's thumb traces my cheekbone. "She's still here. But not because you're delicate. Because you're strong enough to be both. Grace and resilience. Beauty and steel."

I kiss him again, and this time it's not desperate. It's claiming. His hands slide down to my thighs, lift me up, and my legs wrap around his waist instinctively. He carries me to the couch, lays me down with surprising gentleness, given how hard we're both breathing.

His mouth trails down my neck, across my collarbone, and I arch into him, my hands in his hair, pulling him closer. The dog tags swing forward, cool metal against my heated skin, and I catch them. Hold them.

"Sofia's?" I ask.

"Yeah."

"You wear them every day."

"Every day for five years."

"Why?"

He lifts his head and looks at me. "Because I made the wrong choice." He stops, swallows hard. "Because I needed to remember what happens when protocol matters more than people."

I trace the chain, feel the worn edges of the tags. "And tonight?"

"Tonight I'm choosing differently."

"Even if it costs you everything?"

"Yeah. Even then."

I pull him down, kiss him deep and slow, and feel him surrender to it. His weight settles over me, solid and grounding, and for the first time in three days, I feel safe. Not because we're actually safe—we're not, we're probably more exposed than ever. But because I'm not alone anymore.

His hands find the button of my jeans, and I arch my hips to help him. We're moving fast—probably too fast—but I don't want to slow down. Don't want to think. Just want to feel.

"Maggie—" He pauses, his hand on my waist, his breathing ragged. "We should—"

"It's going to take time for them to come back and try again," I whisper fiercely, my fingers digging into his arms. "Until then, give me this. Give me you."

He searches my eyes for a beat, something raw flickering there, then nods once, sharp and decisive. "Okay."

His mouth crashes back to mine, silencing any lingering doubt, and his fingers make quick work of my jeans, shoving them down my hips along with my underwear in one rough tug.

I kick them off impatiently, exposed now under the dim ranch light, my skin prickling with anticipation as he sheds his own pants, the fabric pooling on the floor. I reach for him, wrapping my hand around his length—hot, thick, pulsing under my grip—and he hisses through his teeth, hips jerking forward into my touch.

I stroke him slowly at first, teasing, watching his jaw clench and his eyes darken, but he doesn't let me lead for long; he pins my wrists gently but firmly above my head, his free hand sliding between my thighs, fingers parting me, finding me slick and aching.

"God, Maggie," he growls against my lips, circling my clit with his thumb in lazy, deliberate strokes that make my breath stutter, my body clenching around nothing, desperate for more.

He dips lower, one finger slipping inside me, then two, curling just right, and I buck against his hand, a whine escaping my throat as he works me open, slow and torturous, building the heat until I'm trembling, so close, teetering on that exquisite edge—but he pulls back, denying me, his touch vanishing just as the coil tightens unbearably.

"Colt, please—" I gasp, frustration twisting deliciously with need, my hips grinding up against empty air.

"Not yet," he murmurs, voice rough as gravel, and then he's there—nudging against my entrance, teasing with shallow thrusts that promise everything but deliver only the tip, stretching me just enough to make me ache deeper, wilder.

I wrap my legs around him, trying to pull him in, but he holds back, controlling the pace, dragging it out until I'm a writhing mess beneath him, every nerve screaming for release, the denial sharpening every sensation until it borders on agony.

Finally, when I'm begging in broken whispers, he surges forward in one deep, claiming thrust, burying himself to the hilt, and I cry out, the fullness overwhelming, perfect.

"Fuuuuuck, you feel so good." He stills for a moment, letting me adjust, our breaths mingling hot and fast, then he starts moving—slow at first, deliberate rolls of his hips that grind against that spot inside me, building the pressure again, higher this time, torturously close without tipping over.

His mouth finds my breast, tongue flicking over my nipple, teeth grazing just enough to send sparks racing down my spine, and I arch into him, nails raking his back as he picks up speed, thrusts turning harder, deeper, the couch groaning under the force.

The world blurs to this rhythm—his body slamming into mine, sweat-slick skin sliding, the wet sounds of us mingling with our ragged moans. I'm right there again, hovering on the brink, every muscle taut, and he senses it, shifts his angle, driving in relentlessly until I shatter—climax crashing over me in waves, my walls clenching around him, pulling him under with me as he groans my name, low and broken, spilling hot inside me with a final, shuddering thrust.

We collapse together, his weight a welcome anchor as aftershocks ripple through me. He rolls us slightly, tucking me against his chest, and I nuzzle into the crook of his neck, inhaling the salt of his skin, the dog tags cool against my cheek.

His arms wrap around me, one hand stroking lazy circles on my back, and for a stolen moment, we just breathe—snuggled close on the worn couch, hearts slowing in tandem, the storm outside a distant rumble.

But he's not done.

Before I can fully catch my breath, he shifts, pressing a kiss to my forehead, then my lips, then lower—trailing hot and open-mouthed down my body. Surprise flares through me as he hooks my thigh over his shoulder, settling between my legs with a hunger in his eyes that makes my pulse kick up again.

"Colt—"

"Shh," he says, voice husky, and then his mouth is on me—tongue delving in without preamble, vigorous and unrelenting, lapping at my oversensitive folds like he's starved for it.

I gasp, fingers fisting in his hair as he sucks my clit between his lips, flicking with precise, teasing pressure that reignites the fire low in my belly, faster this time, reckless and intense.

His hands grip my hips, holding me down as I buck against his face, the stubble on his jaw scraping deliciously against my thighs, his groans vibrating through me as he devours me, tongue thrusting inside before circling back, building me up swiftly and mercilessly. I'm moaning openly now, lost in the wet heat of his mouth, chasing that peak again when—

The perimeter alarm SCREAMS through the moment, harsh and immediate.

We both freeze, hearts pounding for entirely different reasons now.

"Shit, that was faster than I thought." Colt is off me in an instant, reaching for his weapon first and then his clothes, his training overriding everything else.

I'm right behind him, grabbing my clothes and the AR-15, my body shifting from want to combat mode so fast it makes me dizzy.

He's at the window, night vision down. "Multiple vehicles. Head-lights off."

"How many?"

"Can't tell yet. At least two. Maybe more."

I move to my position, weapon up, hands steady despite the adrenaline still singing through my veins from what we were doing. My shirt is back on but inside out, my jeans barely buttoned, and I can still feel the ghost of his hands on my skin.

But that doesn't matter now.

More enforcers are coming, and we have to be ready.

"You good?" Colt asks without looking away from the window.

"Yeah." My voice is steadier than it should be. "I'm good."

"No regrets?"

"About which part?"

"Any of it."

I think about his hands on me. His mouth on mine. The way he said my full name like it was something precious instead of some-thing I should be ashamed of.

"No regrets," I tell him. "You?"

"No regrets." He shifts position, counts. "Two vehicles. They're staging again. Shit, three vehicles."

"So we do it again."

"Yeah. We do it again."

I settle into position, sight through the window, and wait.

This time, I'm not just fighting for survival.

I'm fighting for the right to choose. To be whoever I want to be —Magnolia or Maggie or something in between.

I'm fighting because Coulten Harrison chose me over protocol, and I'll be damned if I let the cartel prove him wrong.

The vehicles start moving forward.

"Here we go," Colt says quietly.

And I'm ready.

SEVEN

FROST

———

THREE VEHICLES. MOVING THROUGH THE DARKNESS, HEADLIGHTS cut low to avoid silhouetting against the dunes, but I've already clocked them from the ridge's edge, scopes pulling their dust trails into sharp focus.

Depending on how they're manned, we're looking at a minimum of three, max of twelve men—reinforcements for the eight idiots we dropped earlier, the cartel's way of saying they don't take failure lightly.

I knew they'd come; hell, I was counting on it. It's why what just happened on that couch was a bad idea from the start—protocol screaming in my skull, every tactical bone in me yelling to keep sharp, keep distant, keep her safe by not getting sloppy with distractions.

But I don't regret it.

Not a goddamn second. Magnolia curled against me, all fire and need and that fierce surrender in her eyes? That was the first real thing I've let myself grab hold of since Sofia, since I locked down and let the world turn gray.

Fucking Magnolia was reckless, yeah, buried deep in her heat, chasing that edge together, then going back for more with my mouth on her until she was trembling again.

Worth every risked minute, every beat of vulnerability, because in that stolen haze we weren't targets or ghosts—we were alive, connected, and it burned away five years of ice in my veins.

Let them come. I'll fight for this now, too.

Even if the odds suck.

I'm at the window with night vision down, counting weapons, assessing formation, cataloging threats with the cold efficiency that comes from a decade of doing this. But my hands are still warm from touching Maggie, and I can still taste her on my lips, and that's a problem.

Can't be thinking about how she felt under my hands when killers are closing in.

Can't be distracted by the way she said my name—Colt, not Frost—when I need to be tactical and sharp and focused on keeping her alive.

But I am distracted. For the first time in five years, since Sofia died and I started wearing her dog tags like penance, I'm distracted by something other than ghosts.

By someone who's still breathing.

"They're spreading out," I say, forcing my voice steady and professional. "Three-man teams. I count nine." But I know there's more. I feel it in my gut.

Maggie moves to her window position, weapon up, and I catch her profile in the dim light—hair still messed from my hands, shirt inside out, lips swollen from my mouth. But her hands are rock-steady on the AR-15, her breathing controlled, her focus absolute.

Combat mode. Just like me.

Except I'm having a hell of a time staying in combat mode when five minutes ago I was memorizing the taste of her skin.

"Rules of engagement?" She's asking it like we're on patrol, like this is just another op, but I can hear the slight breathlessness under-lying the words.

She's feeling it too. The shift. The way everything just changed between us.

"Same as before." I sight down my rifle, tracking the first team's movement. "Kill. No hostages. We don't let them take you."

"Copy that."

The simplicity of it grounds me. I know how to do *this*. I'm trained for it. Keep the asset safe. Eliminate threats. Complete the mission.

Except Maggie stopped being an asset somewhere between the warehouse and right now, and that's the problem.

The first team reaches the barn. They're using it for cover, preparing to advance on the ranch house from the north. Smart. It gives them concealment and a shorter approach to our position.

The second team is circling wide to the south, staying low, using the natural terrain—rocks and scrub brush—for cover. Also smart. They're going to try to pin us in a crossfire.

"They're boxing us in," Maggie observes, her tone clinical. "North and south approach. Force us to split our attention."

"Yeah." I'm already calculating angles, fields of fire, and probable assault vectors. "They want to overwhelm us. Make us choose which threat to engage while the other team breaches."

"So what's our play?"

Our. Not my.

Our play.

Like we're a team.

Like she's not a civilian I pulled out of a warehouse three hours ago, but an operator I've served with for years.

And the hell of it is, she moves like one. Thinks like one. The Army trained her well.

"We make them commit," I tell her. "Let them get close enough to think they have an advantage. Then we hit them hard before they can coordinate."

"That's a narrow window."

"Yeah. But it's what we've got." I shift position, check the south approach. "You take north. I've got south. Fire on my mark."

"Understood."

The teams advance. Fifty meters. Forty. Using cover effectively, moving in bounds—one man covering while the others advance. Professional.

These aren't street-level cartel soldiers.

These are trained operators. Military background, probably. Mexican Special Forces gone private, or ex-military hired for specialized work.

Which means they're dangerous.

Thirty meters.

My finger rests on the trigger, breathing controlled, heart rate steady despite the adrenaline. Despite the fact that twenty minutes ago I was kissing Maggie like I was drowning.

Twenty-five meters.

Focus. Threat assessment. Target priority.

The lead tango on the south team raises his hand. Signal to advance.

"Mark," I say quietly, and squeeze the trigger.

The suppressed round drops the lead tango. I shift, acquire the second target, and fire again. He goes down hard.

Maggie's rifle cracks twice from her window—louder, unsuppressed—and I hear the distinctive sound of bodies hitting dirt.

Four down.

But these men are good. They scatter immediately, taking hard cover, returning fire that forces us back from the windows. Rounds punch through the walls, kicking up concrete dust, too close.

"They know our positions," Maggie calls over the gunfire. "We need to move."

She's right. Staying static gets you killed.

"North window," I tell her. "Move on my cover fire."

I lay down suppressing fire on the remaining tangos, forcing them to keep their heads down. Maggie moves fast and low, in a combat crouch, weapon ready, reaching the north window and taking up position in three seconds flat.

The Army trained her *very* well.

She engages immediately. Her weapon fires twice. Once. Once more.

"Two more down," she reports, her voice controlled despite the adrenaline I know must be screaming through her system. "That's six total."

Six tangos down. No casualties on our side.

But it's not over.

"Too easy," I mutter, scanning the perimeter through night vision. "They sent six operators against two targets in a defended position. That's either arrogance or—"

The sound of another engine rumbling in the distance answers my question.

"Or a first wave," Maggie finishes. "Testing our defenses. Seeing what we're capable of."

"Yeah." I count headlights approaching. "And here comes the second wave."

But it's not multiple vehicles this time. Just one. Single sedan, expensive, moving slowly up the access road like whoever's driving isn't worried about an ambush.

Like they think they have leverage.

My gut clenches with recognition before my brain catches up. I know that vehicle. Saw it in the surveillance footage my contact sent.

Tyler Brooks's Tesla.

"Maggie." My voice comes out harder than I intend. "North window. Now."

She moves to my position, looks where I'm pointing, and her entire body goes rigid beside me.

"That's Tyler's car." Her voice is flat. Empty. The kind of empty that comes right before breaking. "That's his car."

"Yeah."

"He's here." She's gripping the rifle so hard her knuckles are white. "He actually came here. Helped them find me and then came to—what? Watch? Collect his payout?"

"I don't know." But I have a pretty good idea, and none of the options are good.

The Tesla stops a hundred yards out. The driver's door opens. Tyler Brooks steps out, hands raised, performing again. Even from this distance, I can see the expensive watch, the designer jacket, the confident posture of someone who thinks he's in control.

Who thinks he's safe.

"Maggie!" He calls out, voice carrying across the desert. "Maggie, I know you're in there! Just—let me explain, okay? This is all a huge misunderstanding!"

Beside me, Maggie is shaking. Not from fear. From rage.

"A misunderstanding." She breathes the words like poison. "He sold me to a cartel, and it's a misunderstanding?"

"Don't engage," I tell her. "Let him talk. See what he reveals."

But she's already moving, standing up in full view of the window, weapon pointed directly at her brother.

"Stop," I start, but she ignores me.

"A misunderstanding?" She shouts it, and her voice is razor-sharp. "Which part, Tyler? The part where you racked up one hundred and eighty thousand in gambling debt? Or the part where you offered me as collateral to a cartel?"

Tyler has the grace to look uncomfortable. "Mags, if you'd just let me explain—"

"Don't call me that." The rifle in her hands doesn't waver. "You don't get to use that name anymore."

"I'm your brother—"

"You were my brother." She takes a step closer to the window, and I can see her finger on the trigger, see the tension in her shoulders. "I spent ten years taking care of you. Making sure you had everything you needed. And you sold me? What kind of brother does that?"

"I was trying to protect you." Tyler's voice rises, defensive. "The cartel was going to kill me if I didn't pay. I had to give them something—"

"So you gave them me."

"I was going to get you out. Once I paid off the debt, once I had the money, I was going to—"

"Liar." The single word cuts through his explanation. "You were never going to get me out. The trust fund was just the bonus. I was always the primary payment."

Tyler's mask cracks. I see it from here—the moment he realizes she knows everything. That she's not the naive older sister he thought he could manipulate anymore.

"How did you—" He stops. "Did he say that? The one who rescued you? How do you know he's not doing the same thing? Maggie, he's lying to you. He's trying to turn you against me. We're family—"

"Family doesn't sell family," Maggie cuts him off. "Family doesn't meet with cartel lieutenants while their sister is being hunted. Family doesn't help track down someone they claim to love so they can hand them over to settle a debt."

"I was trying to make a deal. To get you back safe—"

"You were trying to get paid." Her voice breaks, but the rifle doesn't. "Just admit it, Tyler. For once in your life, admit what you are."

Silence. Long and heavy and damning.

Then Tyler's expression changes. The fake concern drops away, replaced by something uglier. Resentment. Bitterness. The real Tyler emerges from behind the performance.

"You want the truth?" His voice is different now. Sharper. "Fine. You were suffocating me. Always the perfect sister. Always the responsible one. Always making me feel like a fucking failure because you had your shit together and I didn't."

"So you sold me."

"So I took control of my own life." He's shouting now. "That trust fund is half mine. You have no right to keep it from me."

"Two years, Tyler. It's been accessible for two years. And I said no because I knew you'd blow it on exactly the kind of stupid shit that got you into debt in the first place."

"It's my money—"

"It's Mother's legacy." Her voice cracks fully now. "She wanted us to have security. To have something she never had. And you— you gambled it away before you even had it. You sold your own sister to cover your losses."

"I didn't have a choice. They were going to kill you."

"There's always a choice." She's crying now, tears streaming down her face, but her hands are still steady. "You chose gambling over family. You chose debt over doing the right thing. You chose to sell me rather than face the consequences of your own actions."

Tyler's voice cracks. "Maggie, please. You know me. Whatever this man told you—he's lying. He wants to turn you against me. We're family. Family doesn't—"

"Sign over trust document?"

"What?" He blinks.

"That's what you were going to say. Family doesn't abandon each other. Family helps." She raises the rifle. "Yet, here you are with a cartel. You already sold me to them once. Wasn't that enough?"

Silence

His expression flickers—confusion, then calculation, then something ugly.

"You always thought you were better than me. Saint Maggie, who joined the Army. Perfect Maggie, who sacrificed everything. Well, guess what? You're not perfect. You're not even smart. You really thought I'd let you control my life forever?"

"I was taking care of you."

"I didn't ask you to." He's screaming now. "I didn't ask you to give up college. I didn't ask you to join the Army. I didn't ask you to treat me like a child for ten years."

"You were seventeen when Mother died—"

"And you made sure I never forgot it. Made sure I knew that everything I had was because of you. That I owed you. That I was the burden you had to carry." His face is red, spittle flying. "Well, I'm done being your burden. I'm done being the little brother you get to fix. Maybe Mother should have just left everything to you since you're so fucking perfect—"

A gunshot cracks through the night.

Tyler drops, screaming, clutching his shoulder. Blood blooms dark against his expensive jacket.

Maggie's rifle is smoking.

I'd move to her if I could, but I can't afford to give away my position. But she's steady. Controlled. Her breathing is even, her grip on the weapon professional.

She shot to disable, not to kill. Shoulder wound. Painful but not fatal. The shot of someone who's trained. Who knows exactly what they're doing.

"You don't get to talk about Mother." Her voice is quiet now. Deadly calm. "You don't get to use her as an excuse for what you became."

Tyler writhes on the dust-choked ground outside the window, his curses a ragged stream of venom as blood soaks through his pant leg. "You shot me. You fucking shot me."

"Yeah. I did." Maggie lowers the rifle, her voice steady but edged with ice. "And I could have gone center mass. Could have killed you. I chose not to. That's more mercy than you showed me."

She turns away from the window, from her brother, and her face is completely empty—shock settling in like frost, adrenaline crashing hard now that the reality of putting a bullet in her own blood slams home.

I reach for her, instinct overriding the mess in my head, but she holds up a hand. "I'm fine."

"You're not fine."

"I'm functional." She sets the rifle down carefully on the scarred table. "That's all that matters right now."

Before I can push back, I hear it: the distinctive thump of rotors slicing the pre-dawn air, helicopters approaching fast. Multiple birds —heavy transport, by the low growl. My gut twists, but not from fear.

I pull out my phone and check the screen. Message from CJ.

TRACKED YOUR SAT PHONE. EN ROUTE. ETA 90 SECONDS. YOU'RE IN DEEP SHIT, FROST.

Guardian HRS. Finally mobilized. Finally here.

Relief and dread hit simultaneously. Relief because backup means safety. Means extraction. It means Maggie will be protected properly.

Dread because backup also means accountability. Means I have to face CJ. Means my unauthorized op, my solo rescue, my complete disregard for protocol just caught up with me.

Two Guardian SUVs roar up the access road, tires kicking up

gravel in a storm of dust, followed by the helicopters sweeping overhead with searchlights stabbing the darkness like accusatory fingers.

Four operators exit each vehicle in tactical formation, weapons up—suppressed M4s sweeping the perimeter, night-vision goggles casting their faces in eerie green glows as they scan for threats.

More rappel down from the helicopters, black-clad figures dropping like shadows, boots hitting the ground with muffled thuds before they fan out.

CJ himself steps out of the lead vehicle. Mid-forties, built like he still runs marathons, expression hard enough to cut glass. He's wearing full tactical gear despite the fact that it's oh-four-hundred, which means he dropped everything and mobilized the second he figured out where I was.

He does not look happy.

But before he can bark orders, the remaining six cartel goons—flankers who'd peeled off from the vehicles during the initial rush, trying to circle the ranch—reveal themselves in a desperate bid, bursting from cover behind the derelict barn and corrals, AKs chattering in sporadic bursts that light up the night.

Bullets ping off the SUVs' armored sides, shattering a rotted fence post nearby, but the Guardians are already moving, a symphony of lethal efficiency.

"Contact left. Six tangos." Max, lead Guardian of Alpha team, snaps over the comms, voice calm as he drops to a knee and pops two suppressed rounds—headshots, clean and instant, the men crumpling like ragdolls before they can fully acquire targets.

Alpha team flows like water. Two Guardians peel right—flanking the barn, their thermal up. Flashbang crack, followed by a burst of fire that silences the frantic shouts inside.

Bodies hit the dirt, no return fire, the acrid tang of cordite drifting on the wind.

Maggie tenses beside me, hand twitching toward the rifle, but I shake my head. "They're handling it."

The last pair of cartel fighters makes a break for the dunes, scrambling for their stalled truck, but the helicopter spotlights pin them like insects, and rappelling operators touch down twenty yards out, advancing in bounding overwatch. A quick exchange—three rounds total—and it's over, the men face-down in the sand, no drama, no mercy.

"Area clear," a voice crackles over the open channel, the team sweeping the ranch in overlapping sectors: checking the outbuildings, the vehicles, even under the porch. Drones buzz overhead for aerial confirmation, and within ninety seconds, another call: *"All clear. Perimeter secure. No additional hostiles."*

After the firefight ends, silence falls. Not the waiting-for-violence silence. The after-violence void. The kind that means it's over.

The tension bleeds out of the air, replaced by the low murmur of post-op check-ins.

"Frost!" CJ's voice carries across the distance, sharp as a blade. "Step outside."

I look at Maggie. She's pale, shocky, but her eyes are clear. "Go. I'm fine."

"Stay inside," I tell her. "Cover the window. Just in case."

"In case of what? Your own team?"

"In case Tyler's friends are still out there." I move toward the door. "Stay sharp."

I step outside, hands visible, weapon slung. CJ approaches with two operators flanking him, and his face is a mask of controlled fury.

"You want to tell me what the hell you've been doing?" He's not shouting, which is worse. CJ only gets quiet when he's genuinely pissed. "Unauthorized op. No communication. Six dead cartel enforcers and one wounded civilian. You've been dark for six hours, Frost. Six hours."

"I can explain—"

"You better have one hell of an explanation." He looks past me to the ranch house. "Is the package secure?"

"Magnolia Brooks. Yeah. She's secure."

"Injuries?"

"Head wound from initial capture. Minor. She's ambulatory and combat-effective."

CJ's eyebrow rises. "Combat-effective?"

"Former Army combat medic. She engaged and dropped multiple tangos during the assault. Took out two trucks on the road."

"A civilian engaged?" His voice gets quieter. Colder. "You armed a civilian and put her in a firefight?"

"I armed a trained soldier who was the primary target. She's qualified to defend herself."

"That's not your call to make."

"It was when I was the only one here." I meet his eyes. "I considered calling it in, but Guardian HRS couldn't mobilize fast enough. She had three hours before the cartel moved her. I did what had to be done."

"By going completely dark. By violating your leave status. By conducting an unauthorized solo rescue operation that could have gotten you killed." CJ steps closer. "You went rogue, Frost. Again. Just like Caracas."

"This isn't Caracas."

"Isn't it?" His eyes are hard. "Solo op. No backup. Making it personal. You see the pattern?"

"In Caracas, I followed orders, and someone died. This time, I broke orders, and someone lived. You tell me which one was wrong."

"Both," CJ snaps. "They were both wrong because you keep making it about your guilt instead of the mission. You wear Sofia's dog tags and then wonder why you can't let anything go."

His words hit harder than they should because he's not wrong.

"The civilian—Maggie," CJ continues. "She needs medical assessment, debriefing, and witness protection. The wounded hostile —" He glances at Tyler, still bleeding on the ground, being treated by one of our medics. "—needs transport to federal custody. And you need to come with me for a very long conversation about why I shouldn't terminate your contract right now."

"Understood."

"Do you?" He leans in, voice dropping. "Because from where I'm standing, you just threw away your career for a woman you met six hours ago. And I need to know if that was worth it."

I look back at the ranch house. Maggie is at the window, watching us, weapon still ready. Even from here, I can see the set of her shoulders, the way she's holding herself together through sheer will.

She shot her own brother twenty minutes ago. Disabled him rather than killed him, which took more control than most trained operators have. And now she's standing guard like a professional because that's who she is when everything falls apart.

Strong. Capable. Fierce.

Worth saving.

Worth choosing.

"Yeah," I tell CJ. "It was worth it, and to be honest, she'd make a fine Guardian. You ever think of hiring a woman, she should be first on your list."

His expression doesn't change, but something flickers in his eyes. Understanding, maybe. Or resignation.

"Federal agent is en route," he says finally. "Witness protection coordinator. Maggie Brooks will be relocated within the hour. New identity. New life. You won't see her again."

The words land like a physical blow.

Won't see her again.

I knew that was coming. Knew witness protection meant disappearing. Knew that saving her life meant losing whatever this is between us before it even had a chance to start.

But knowing doesn't make it hurt less.

"Frost?" CJ's voice pulls me back. "You hearing me?"

"Yeah. I hear you."

"Good. Now get your head straight and help me secure this scene. We've got six bodies, one wounded hostile, and a shitstorm of paperwork coming our way."

"Twelve."

"Excuse me?"

"There are twelve bodies. That's the second wave." I point vaguely toward the darkness where the bodies of the first wave lie.

"Fuck me." He turns to his operators. "Document everything. And someone get that civilian out here for medical assessment."

I watch them move, efficient and professional, taking control of a situation I created by going rogue. Again.

CJ's right. I do keep making it personal. Keep choosing people over protocol. Keep breaking rules because I can't get past Caracas, can't get past Sofia, can't get past the guilt of following orders while someone died.

But this time someone lived.

Maggie lived.

And in an hour, she'll disappear into witness protection, and I'll never see her again, and that was always how this was going to end.

I just didn't expect it to feel like losing something I never actually had.

Maggie emerges from the ranch house, weapon slung, moving with that same controlled competence that's defined every interaction since I cut her loose. One of our medics approaches, starts checking her over, and she submits to the exam with professional patience.

Her eyes find mine across the distance.

Even from here, I can see the question in them. *What happens now?*

I don't have an answer that doesn't involve watching her walk away.

CJ claps a hand on my shoulder. "Come on. Let's debrief. And Frost? Whatever you're feeling right now? Lock it down. She's a witness, you're an operator, and this is over."

But it doesn't feel over.

It feels like it's just beginning.

EIGHT

MAGGIE

The Guardian medic is efficient and impersonal, checking my pupils with a penlight that makes my head throb worse.

"Concussion is mild," he says, fingers probing the wound on my temple. "You're lucky. Another inch and that pistol-whip could have fractured your skull."

Lucky. Right.

I'm standing in the pre-dawn darkness watching my brother get loaded into an SUV with a gunshot wound I gave him, while the man who saved my life gets dressed down by his team leader fifty yards away, and in an hour I'll disappear into witness protection with a new name and a new life and no way back to any of this.

Tyler's eyes find mine across the distance. Even bleeding, even beaten, there's no remorse in them. Just resentment.

"You always thought you were better than me," he says, loud enough to carry.

I wait for the grief to hit. The sisterly love. The hope he'll apologize.

Nothing comes.

"I am better than you," I say quietly, not caring if he hears me. "Because I would never have sold you."

The medic continues his exam.

"Any nausea? Dizziness? Vision problems?" The medic is going through the checklist like I'm not actively dissociating.

"No. I'm fine."

"You're not fine. You're in shock." He wraps a blood pressure cuff around my arm. "Elevated heart rate. Shallow breathing. Pupils dilated. When's the last time you ate?"

I try to remember. The warehouse. Three days ago. They gave me water but no food. Said I needed to stay alert to sign the papers.

To sign away my life.

"Three days," I hear myself say.

The medic swears under his breath. "We need to get fluids and glucose into you. You're running on adrenaline and spite."

Spite.

That's accurate.

I look past him to where Colt is standing with CJ. Even from here, I can read the tension in Colt's shoulders, the rigid set of his spine. He's being taken apart professionally, and there's nothing I can do about it.

He went rogue for me. Violated orders. Risked his career. Saved my life.

And now he's paying for it while I stand here getting my blood pressure taken like any of this matters.

"Ms. Brooks." A new voice. Female, professional, carrying a badge. "I'm Special Agent Holbrook, FBI. I need to ask you some questions."

The medic protests. "She needs medical treatment first—"

"She needs to give her statement while the details are fresh." Agent Holbrook's expression is sympathetic but firm. "It won't take long."

I walk her through everything. The staged kidnapping. Tyler's debt. The trust fund. The warehouse. Colt's extraction. The ranch house. The two assaults. Shooting Tyler.

She takes notes without judgment, asks clarifying questions, and records everything on a digital device that will probably end up in a federal database somewhere.

"And the Guardian operative—Frost—he acted alone throughout?" She's watching me carefully when she asks this.

"Yes."

"No authorization from Guardian HRS?"

"He was on leave. He overheard cartel members talking in a bar and followed them."

"That was fortunate."

"That was brave." I meet her eyes. "He saved my life when nobody else could have gotten there in time."

Something flickers in Agent Holbrook's expression. Understanding, maybe. "Your statement corroborates his version of events. That'll help."

"Will he lose his job?"

"That's not my jurisdiction. But off the record?" She leans in slightly. "Guardian HRS values results. Twelve dead cartel enforcers and a rescued hostage are good results, unauthorized or not."

It's not much reassurance, but it's something.

Agent Holbrook closes her tablet. "The witness protection coordinator will be here within the hour. I understand this is overwhelming, but the cartel's still active and they've already demonstrated they're willing to commit significant resources to recovering you."

"I'm not a product." The words come out harder than I intend. "I'm not inventory or an asset or something to be recovered. I'm a person."

"I know." Her voice softens. "And we're going to keep you safe. New identity, new location, full support until the threat is neutralized."

"How long?"

"Minimum two years. Possibly longer depending on cartel activity."

Two years?

Minimum?

Two years of being someone else. Somewhere else. No contact with anyone from before.

Including Colt?

"Your brother will face federal charges," Agent Holbrook continues. "Human trafficking, conspiracy, fraud. He's cooperating, which will help his sentencing, but he's looking at a minimum of fifteen years."

Fifteen years. Tyler will be in his forties when he gets out. If he gets out.

I should feel something about that. Sadness. Relief. Anger. Something.

But I'm empty.

Agent Holbrook leaves, and I'm alone again. The medic returns with an IV bag, insists on getting fluids into me, and I let him because it's easier than arguing. The needle slides into my arm, and the cool liquid begins to flow. I watch the eastern horizon lighten as the approaching dawn breaks.

Six hours ago, I was zip-tied to a chair in a warehouse, believing my brother was a victim like me.

Three hours ago, I learned the truth about what Tyler did.

One hour ago, I kissed Colt Harrison like he was the only real thing in a world made of lies.

Twenty minutes ago, I shot my brother.

And in forty minutes I'll disappear.

"Maggie." CJ's voice pulls me out of my spiral. He's approaching alone; Colt is nowhere in sight. "Got a minute?"

"Do I have a choice?"

"Not really." But his tone isn't unkind. He sits down on the tailgate of the Guardian SUV beside me, and up close, I can see the exhaustion in his face. "Hell of a night."

"Yeah."

"Frost gave me his version of events. Now I need yours."

"Agent Holbrook already took my statement."

"This isn't about the FBI. This is about Frost." CJ looks at me directly. "He violated protocol. Went dark. Conducted an unauthorized solo rescue operation. That's grounds for termination."

My stomach clenches. "He saved my life."

"I know."

"The cartel would have moved me in three hours. Guardian HRS couldn't mobilize that fast. He did what had to be done."

"I know that too." CJ runs his hand over his face. "But I need to understand something. When he armed you and put you in a firefight—was that his call or yours?"

"Mine. I grabbed his weapon and took out the trucks following us. After that, he armed me when we got here, but I'm a former Army. Combat medic. I know how to handle a weapon."

"That's not the point. The point is whether he was thinking tactically or emotionally."

"Both." I pull the IV out of my arm, ignore the medic's protest. "He was thinking tactically because I'm trained and capable. He was thinking emotionally because he gives a damn whether I live or die. Those aren't mutually exclusive."

CJ studies me for a long moment. "You have feelings for him."

It's not a question.

"I've known him for six hours."

"That's not an answer."

I look toward the ranch house where Colt is helping operators document the scene. Even from here, I can see the efficiency of his movements, the way he's compartmentalized everything to focus on the mission.

"He wears dog tags that aren't his," I say finally. "From a woman who died in Caracas five years ago because he followed orders instead of choosing to protect her. He's been punishing himself ever since. Wearing guilt like armor."

"Sofia." CJ's voice is quiet. "We were both CIA at the time. I was his team leader on that op. The call to extract without her came from CIA command. Frost followed my orders."

"And someone died."

"Yeah. Someone died." CJ leans back against the SUV. "I left the CIA and joined Guardian HRS soon after. Frost followed me. He's a damn good operator. But he's been making every decision since then based on that guilt. Going rogue. Making it personal. Choosing people over protocol."

"Is that wrong?"

"It is when it gets operators killed. When it compromises missions. When it—" He stops. "When it makes him reckless."

"He wasn't reckless. He was precise. Professional. Tactical." I meet CJ's eyes. He chose to save someone rather than let stupid protocols get in the way. That's not reckless. That's brave."

"Brave or not, it has consequences."

"Like what? Termination? For saving my life?"

"Like mandatory psychological evaluation. Like suspension pending review. Like—" CJ's expression softens slightly. "Like me having to decide if he's fit for duty or if his guilt is going to get him killed on the next op."

The implications settle over me like a lead weight. Colt didn't just risk his career. He risked everything. His job. His team. His life. Maybe even his sanity.

For me.

For a woman he didn't know and met six hours ago.

"He's fit for duty," I tell CJ. "He's one of the best operators I've seen, and I served with some exceptional soldiers."

"You're biased."

"So are you. You're his team leader. You're supposed to be biased in favor of your people."

CJ almost smiles. "Fair point." He stands, stretches. "Witness protection coordinator will be here in twenty. You'll be relocated immediately. New identity, new location, no contact with your former life."

"I know."

"That includes Frost."

"I know."

"Once you're in the program, you can't reach out. Can't make contact. It compromises security." He looks at me directly. "You understand what that means?"

It means losing Colt before I ever figured out what this is between us.

It means disappearing into a new life while he stays here, dealing with the consequences of saving mine.

It means never knowing if he's okay, if CJ terminates him, or if his guilt finally consumes him.

"I understand," I manage.

CJ nods, starts to walk away, then pauses. "For what it's worth? I think he made the right call. Even if it was for the wrong reasons."

"What are the right reasons?"

"Saving a life. That's always the right reason." He glances back toward where Colt is working. "The wrong reason was thinking that saving your life would absolve him of Sofia's death. That's not how guilt works."

He walks away before I can respond.

I sit there on the tailgate, IV bag dripping unused beside me, watching the sky lighten from black to gray to the pale blue of approaching dawn.

The desert is quiet now, the violence of the night fading into the mundane work of cleanup. Bodies are being photographed and documented. Shell casings collected. Statements recorded.

My brother is being transported to federal custody.

My life is being erased so a new one can be built from nothing.

"Maggie." Colt's voice is quiet, close. He's standing a few feet away, hands in his pockets, looking uncertain in a way I haven't seen from him before. "Can we talk?"

"They told you not to."

"Yeah. CJ said it compromises security. That I need to let you go." He moves closer. "But, I'm terrible at following orders."

Despite everything, I almost smile. "I noticed."

He sits down beside me on the tailgate, and the warmth of him is immediate and familiar. His shoulder brushes mine, and I feel the contact like electricity.

"Agent Holbrook said witness protection," he says quietly. "New identity. No contact."

"Yeah."

"How long?"

"Two years minimum."

He's quiet for a long moment. "That's a long time."

"Yeah."

"Maggie—" He stops, starts again. "I need to tell you something before you go."

I look at him. His face is shadowed in the pre-dawn light,

exhaustion etched into every line. The dog tags are visible at his collar, Sofia's tags that he's worn for five years.

"You don't owe me anything," I tell him. "You saved my life. That's enough."

"It's not about owing. It's about—" He runs his hand through his hair, frustrated. "CJ thinks I saved you to assuage my guilt about Sofia. That I'm trying to rewrite Caracas by making different choices."

"Are you?"

"At first, maybe. When I heard those men talking in the bar, when I decided to follow them—yeah. I was thinking about Sofia. About choosing differently." He turns to face me fully. "But then I found you in that warehouse. And you made a joke about my scowl. And you kept pace during extraction like you'd been running ops for years. And you shot your own brother to protect yourself while still having the control not to kill him."

"Colt—"

"And somewhere between the warehouse and right now, this stopped being about Sofia." His hand comes up, cups my face with surprising gentleness. His thumb traces the bandage on my temple. "This became about you. About Maggie Brooks, who survived being sold by her own brother. About Magnolia, who's strong and fierce and doesn't break even when everything falls apart."

My throat is tight. "You're making this harder."

"I know. But you need to hear it before you disappear." He reaches up and pulls the dog tags over his head. Sofia's tags. The ones he's worn every day for five years. "These belonged to someone I couldn't save. Someone who died because I followed orders instead of choosing her."

"I know."

"I've worn them as penance. As a reminder. As punishment for making the wrong choice." He holds them out to me. "But I'm done punishing myself for Caracas. I'm done wearing guilt like armor. And you're the reason why."

I stare at the tags in his palm. "I can't take those."

"Yes, you can and you will."

"They're Sofia's—"

"They're a reminder that I made the wrong choice once." He takes my hand, places the tags in my palm, and closes my fingers around them. "And I'm not making it again. I'm choosing you. I chose you in that warehouse. I chose you at the ranch. I'm choosing you now."

"I'm about to disappear for two years."

"I know."

"You'll never see me again."

"That's not true." He pulls something from his pocket. Two cards. "This one—" He hands me the first card, white with printed text. "—is Guardian HRS official emergency line. Twenty-four-seven response. Someone will always answer. They're good. They'll help. I may, or may not, have told CJ he should hire you."

I take it, feel the weight of professional support. Of an organization that saves people.

"And this one—" He hands me the second card. Blank except for a handwritten phone number. "—is not official. Not Guardian HRS. Just me."

I stare at the number. "Colt—"

"You call that number, I come. No matter where you are. No matter what I'm doing. No matter how long it's been." His eyes are intense, absolute. "I come. That's my promise."

"You can't promise that. You don't know where they're sending me. You don't know if you'll even have this number in two years—"

"I'll have it. And I'll answer." He leans in, his forehead resting against mine. "Two years. When your protection detail ends, when you're free—call that number."

"What if I can't? What if something happens and—"

"Then I'll find you." His hand tightens on mine. "I'm very good at finding people who don't want to be found. And you? You're someone I'm never going to stop looking for."

The tags are warm in my palm from his body heat. Five years of him wearing them. Five years of guilt and penance and choosing wrong.

And now he's giving them to me.

"What about Sofia?" My voice cracks. "What about remembering her?"

"I'll remember her by making better choices. By choosing people over protocol. By—" He stops, swallows hard. "By choosing you."

A black sedan pulls up. Federal plates. Witness protection coordinator.

Our time is up.

Colt stands, pulls me to my feet. For a moment, we just stand there, close enough that I can feel the warmth of him, smell the gunpowder and desert dust that clings to us both.

"This isn't goodbye," he says quietly.

"Feels like goodbye."

"It's a pause. Two years. Then you call that number."

"What if you've moved on by then? Found someone else? Decided I was just—"

He kisses me. Hard and fast and absolute. When he pulls back, his eyes are fierce. "I spent five years trying to move on from guilt. I'm not spending two years moving on from you."

The coordinator is approaching, professional and efficient. "Ms. Brooks? We need to go."

I look at Colt one more time, memorizing him. The stubble on his jaw. The shadows under his eyes. The way he's looking at me like I'm something precious instead of a product to be sold.

"Two years," I say. "Deal."

"Two years," he confirms.

I slip the dog tags over my head. They settle against my chest, still warm, carrying the weight of his guilt and his choice and his promise.

Then I turn and walk toward the sedan before I can change my mind.

The coordinator opens the door, and I slide into the back seat. Through the window I can see Colt standing there, hands in his pockets, watching me leave.

CJ approaches him, says something I can't hear. Colt responds without looking away from me.

The sedan starts moving.

I twist in my seat, keeping him in sight as long as possible. He's still standing there, still watching, still choosing me even as I disappear.

The Guardian HRS vehicles fade into the distance. The ranch house. The desert. The bodies and the blood and the violence of the night.

All of it falling away behind me.

"Where are we going?" I ask the coordinator.

"Can't tell you until we arrive. Security protocol." She glances at me in the rearview mirror. "But it's somewhere safe. Somewhere, the cartel can't find you."

Safe. Away from Tyler. Away from the cartel. Away from the life I used to have.

Away from Colt.

My hand finds the dog tags around my neck, and I hold them tight. Sofia's tags. His penance. Now mine to carry.

Two years.

I can survive two years.

I survived Tyler's betrayal. Survived the cartel. Survived learning that family means nothing when gambling debts mean everything.

I can survive missing someone I barely know.

Except I do know him. Know the way he moves in combat. Know the taste of him. Know the sound of my name on his lips—both names, Maggie and Magnolia, like they're both equally real.

Know that he chose me over protocol, over orders, over five years of guilt.

The coordinator is talking about the next steps. About the process. About what happens when we arrive at the safe house. I'm not really listening.

The coordinator reaches for my door, about to close it.

"Wait." I lean out. "Colt."

He's still standing there, hands in pockets, watching me leave.

"Thank you," I call across the distance. Inadequate words for the man who saved my life, gave me truth, and chose me over protocol.

He doesn't respond. Just touches his chest where Sophia's dog tags used to be.

Where I'm wearing them now.

The door closes. We drive away.

I'm already thinking about a phone number on a blank card.

About a promise made in the pre-dawn darkness.

About two years feeling like forever and no time at all.

The sun breaks over the horizon, flooding the desert with gold and pink and the promise of a new day. A new life. A new identity that isn't Magnolia Brooks or Maggie Brooks but someone else entirely.

Someone who carries dog tags that don't belong to her.

Someone who already has a phone number burned into her brain for a lifeline.

Someone who's going to survive the next two years because at the end of them, she's going to make a call.

And Colt Harrison is going to answer.

That's the promise we made.

The one we're both going to keep.

Two years.

I touch the dog tags one more time, feel the worn metal, the engraved name that isn't mine.

Sofia's reminder became Colt's penance, then became my promise.

Some promises are made in silence. In the space between choosing wrong and choosing right. In the moment when someone looks at you and sees a person instead of a product, strength instead of fragility, worth instead of price.

Colt saw me. Really saw me. Not the sister Tyler sold, or the medic who patched up casualties, or the daughter trying to be what her mother wanted.

He saw Magnolia and Maggie and whoever I'm becoming, and he chose all of it.

Two years.

I'm going to survive them.

And then I'm going to call that number.

And he's going to answer.

Because some promises are worth keeping.

And this one—this one I'm going to keep even if it kills me.

The sedan carries me away from the desert, from the violence, from the man who saved my life and changed everything in six hours.

But I'm not gone.

I'm just waiting.

Two years.

Then I'm coming back.

And Colt Harrison better be ready.

Because I'm choosing him too.

NINE

MAGGIE

Six months.

I'm sitting at the kitchen table in my Portland apartment—not my apartment, Emma Richardson's apartment—with cold coffee and the dog tags warm against my chest. Rain streaks the window, typical for November in the Pacific Northwest, and the sky is that particular shade of gray that makes you forget what sunlight looks like.

Emma Richardson serves coffee with a smile that never reaches her eyes.

The regular at table four—the professor who always orders a triple espresso and tips exactly 18%—doesn't notice the smile is fake. Nobody at Roasted Beans notices much about Emma Richardson.

She's pleasant, efficient, and utterly forgettable.

Perfect for witness protection.

The name still feels wrong in my mouth. Like wearing someone else's clothes that almost fit but not quite. I've practiced saying it a thousand times. Written it on forms and applications, and the name tag at the coffee shop where I work mornings. Responded to it when neighbors call out in the hallway.

But I'm not Emma Richardson.

I'm Maggie Brooks. Magnolia Brooks. The woman whose brother sold her to a cartel. The woman who shot him in the shoulder and watched him bleed. The woman who kissed a Guardian operator in an abandoned ranch while a dozen enforcers closed in.

The woman who's been waiting for permission to make a phone call.

Eighteen more months to go.

I wipe down the counter and check the clock: 2:47 PM. Three hours until my shift ends. Then home to my apartment that isn't mine, to cook dinner I don't taste, to watch TV I don't care about, to sleep in a bed where I dream about warehouses and the man who saved me.

The dog tags are heavier today. Or maybe I'm just more aware of them. Sofia's name is engraved in worn metal, a reminder of wrong choices, guilt, and penance. Except they're not penance anymore. They're a promise.

Two years, Colt said. *Then you call that number.*

But it's only been six months, and I'm not allowed to call anyone from before. Not friends. Not former Army buddies. Not the man who saved my life and gave me his promise in the pre-dawn darkness.

At 6:00 PM, I clock out. Walk three blocks to my apartment in the rain. Climb three flights of stairs. Unlock door 3C.

The rain gets heavier, drumming against the window. November in Portland means gray skies, wet streets, and forgetting what sunlight looks like.

I should make dinner. Should eat something. Should pretend Emma Richardson is a real person with a real life.

Instead, I sit at the kitchen table with cold coffee and Sophia's dog tags warm against my chest.

My phone buzzes on the table. Unknown number.

I stare at it for three full rings before I reach for it. Unknown numbers are usually spam. Student loan forgiveness I don't need.

Extended car warranties for a vehicle I don't own. Nobody calls Emma Richardson because Emma Richardson doesn't exist.

But my hand is shaking when I pick it up.

"Hello?"

Silence. Just the faint sound of breathing and rain—not my rain, different rain, somewhere else.

Then: "Magnolia."

My heart stops. Completely stops. Then restarts so hard I feel it in my throat, in my ears, in my fingertips wrapped around the phone.

That voice. Low and rough and saying my name like it's something precious.

"Colt?" I'm on my feet without remembering standing up. "How did you—"

"I kept my promise." His voice is quiet, controlled, but I can hear something underneath it. Relief. Longing. Six months compressed into three words. "I'm outside."

The phone nearly slips from my hand.

Outside. He's outside. Right now.

"You can't be here." But I'm already moving toward the window, looking down at the street three stories below. "The program—the rules—if they find out—"

"I don't care about the rules."

Of course he doesn't. He went rogue for me six months ago. Violated orders. Risked his career. Why would witness protection protocols stop him now?

I see him.

Standing on the sidewalk across from my building, rain soaking through his jacket, phone to his ear, looking up at my window like he knew exactly which one was mine.

Even from three stories up, I can see the way he's standing—hands in pockets except for the one holding the phone, shoulders set with the kind of determination that says he's not leaving until I come down.

"You said two years," I manage, but my voice is breaking.

"I know what I said."

"It's only been six months."

"I know."

"Colt—"

"I couldn't stay away." The words come out rough, raw. "I tried. I made it six months. That's—" He stops. "That's all I could do."

My vision blurs, and I realize I'm crying. Tears mixing with the smile I can't control. "You're going to get me kicked out of the program."

"Then we'll figure something else out."

"That's not how witness protection works—"

"I don't care." His voice gets quieter. More intense. "I spent five years choosing wrong. I'm done with that. I'm choosing you."

Through the rain and the distance, I see him lower the phone slightly, and I do the same, and we're just looking at each other across the space between us.

Six months.

Six months of being Emma Richardson in Portland while Colt Harrison was—where? California? Still with Guardian HRS? Did CJ terminate him? Suspend him? Is he even still an operator, or did saving me cost him everything?

I should ask. Should demand answers. Should be responsible and careful and think about the consequences.

But I'm already grabbing my jacket.

Already shoving my feet into boots.

Already taking the stairs two at a time because the elevator is too slow and Colt is outside and I've been waiting six months for this without even knowing I was allowed to.

The building door swings open, and rain hits my face, cold and sharp and real. He's still standing there across the street, phone in his pocket now, just watching me with those steady eyes that saw through every wall I tried to build.

I don't remember crossing the street. Don't remember the cars or the rain or the distance.

Just his arms coming around me, solid and warm and real.

Just his voice in my ear: "Hi, Magnolia."

Just the way I'm shaking—from cold or relief or six months of holding myself together finally cracking apart.

"You're here." It's all I can manage. "You're actually here."

"Told you I'd come."

"You said two years—"

"I lied." His hand comes up, tangles in my wet hair. "Or I tried to convince myself I could wait two years. Turns out I can't."

I pull back enough to see his face. He looks tired. Thinner than I remember. Dark circles under his eyes, as if he hasn't been sleeping well. But he's here. Real. Solid.

"CJ?" I ask.

"Suspended pending psych eval. Then reinstated with conditions." A ghost of a smile. "Turns out saving hostages is good for Guardian HRS's reputation even when you violate every protocol to do it."

"And the conditions?"

"Mandatory therapy. Regular check-ins. No more solo ops." His hand cups my face. "Worth it."

"You shouldn't be here. If they find out—"

"They won't. I was very careful." He leans his forehead against mine, and I can feel him breathing, feel the solidness of him, feel six months of absence dissolving into right now. "And if they do, we'll figure it out. Together."

"Colt—"

"I'm not asking you to leave the program. I'm not asking you to break the rules or compromise your safety." His thumb traces my cheekbone. "I'm just asking for right now. For this moment. For—"

I kiss him.

Hard and desperate and six months of missing someone I barely knew but couldn't stop thinking about. He kisses back with the same intensity, same need, and we're standing in the rain in Portland and nothing else matters.

When we finally break apart, we're both breathing hard.

"Your apartment. Show me."

We take the stairs again because we can't not be touching, can't maintain the distance the elevator would force. His hand is warm in mine, familiar despite the months apart, and I'm pulling him down the hallway to my door.

Emma Richardson's door.

But when I open it and pull him inside, when he looks around at the sparse furniture and the walls I haven't bothered to decorate because none of this is real—

"It doesn't look like you," he says quietly.

"That's the point."

"Emma Richardson." He says the name like he's testing it. "That who you are now?"

"On paper."

"But not really."

"No. Not really." I touch the dog tags around my neck. "These don't belong to Emma Richardson."

His eyes follow the movement, and something shifts in his expression. "You're still wearing them."

"Every day. Like you did." I meet his gaze. "Reminder of choices. Of promises. Of—"

He crosses the distance between us, and then his mouth is on mine again, and we're stumbling backward toward the couch. His jacket hits the floor. My boots get kicked off somewhere. His hands are under my shirt, and I'm pulling at his, needing skin contact, needing proof this is real.

"Six months," I breathe against his mouth.

"Too long."

"Way too long."

We fall onto the couch in a tangle of limbs and need and six months of wanting compressed into right now. His weight settles over me, perfect and familiar. His mouth finds my throat, and I arch into him, hands sliding under his shirt to feel the muscle and warmth and scars I remember from before.

"Colt—"

"Yeah?"

"How long do you have?"

He lifts his head, looks at me with dark eyes. "As long as you need."

"I need—" Everything. Nothing. This. "I need you not to disappear again."

"I'm not disappearing." His hand cups my face. "I'm right here. For as long as you'll let me stay."

"The program—"

"Doesn't dictate my life. Or yours." He leans in, his forehead resting against mine. "We'll figure it out, Maggie. Together. But right now—right now I just need this."

So I give it to him.

Give us both this moment where Emma Richardson doesn't exist and the cartel is a distant threat and Guardian HRS protocols don't matter. Where it's just Maggie and Colt and six months of missing each other finally ending.

His hands find my face first, cupping it with a tremor that betrays the six months of pent-up longing, fingers shaking as they trace my jaw, my lips, like he's afraid I'll vanish if he doesn't hold on tight enough.

I lean into him, our mouths crashing together in a kiss that's anything but gentle—teeth clashing, nipping at lower lips, his biting down on mine just hard enough to draw a gasp from me, tasting the salt of sweat and the faint copper edge of desperation. It's messy, frantic, tongues tangling as if we could devour the distance that's kept us apart.

"God, Maggie," he growls against my mouth, voice raw, broken with need, and his hands drop to my shirt, yanking at the hem with urgent tugs that bunch the fabric before I help him rip it over my head, my bra following in a tangle of straps.

His shirt's gone in the next heartbeat—buttons straining as we pull in opposite directions, the sound of seams giving way swallowed by our ragged breaths—and then we're skin to skin, chest to chest, the first shock of contact electric after so long without.

His body is furnace-hot against mine, scars rough under my palms as I trace them greedily, mapping the hard planes of muscle that's tensed from months of restraint, the places where old wounds and new tension knot together.

The relief hits like a wave: no more longing through barriers, just this—his heartbeat thundering against my breasts, the faint scratch of his dog tags dragging cool across my ribs, sending shivers racing over my heated skin.

I press closer, nails digging into his shoulders, pulling him down onto me as we stumble toward the bed, clothes shedding in a trail of denim and lace—my jeans kicked off with a hiss of zippers, his belt clattering to the floor.

We're starved, ravenous, hands everywhere at once: mine fisting in his hair to angle his head for deeper kisses that bruise my lips, his sliding down my sides with that lingering shake, gripping my hips hard enough to leave marks, thumbs pressing into the soft give of my thighs as he spreads them, settling between like he belongs there.

Emotional and raw, this isn't just bodies—it's us reclaiming what the separation stole, the trust forged in bullets and betrayal now blooming into something fiercer, his eyes locking on mine between bites and breaths, whispering, "Magnolia," like a vow, then "Maggie," like the truth we've both been chasing.

We move together like we've done this a thousand times instead of just once in an abandoned ranch with violence closing in—slower now amid the frenzy, hips grinding in a rhythm that builds deliberate and deep, but laced with that desperate edge, every thrust a gasp of reconnection.

This is different. No perimeter alarms or incoming threats. Just the rain against the window and the sound of our breathing and the way he says my name—both names, Magnolia and Maggie, like they're equally real, like after all the waiting, we're finally whole.

"I missed you," I hear myself say.

"I know." His mouth finds mine again. "I know because I missed you. Every day. Every call I couldn't make. Every time I wanted to track you down and show up anyway."

"But you waited six months."

"Tried to wait two years. Failed spectacularly." He pulls back enough to look at me. "Does that scare you? That I couldn't stay away?"

"No." I trace his jawline, feel the stubble, the realness of him. "It makes me feel less crazy. Because I've been counting days like a sentence, and it's only been six months, and I already—"

"Already what?"

"Already can't remember why I thought I could wait."

His smile is small but real. "So we're both bad at following rules."

"Apparently."

"Good." He kisses me again, and this time it's not desperate. It's a promise. "I'm done with rules that cost me people I—" He stops.

"People you what?"

"People I care about. People who matter. People who—" He's struggling with the words, and I realize this is hard for him. Admitting feeling. Admitting attachment. "People like you."

It's not a love confession. Too soon for that. Too complicated with witness protection and cartel threats and lives that don't quite fit together yet.

But it's real.

And real is enough.

We stay like that for hours. Talking and kissing and falling asleep tangled together on Emma Richardson's couch. He tells me about the psych eval (passed, barely), about CJ's conditions (annoying but fair), and about the past six months of trying to convince himself he could wait.

I tell him about Portland. About Emma Richardson. About working at a coffee shop and living a life that doesn't fit. About wearing Sophia's dog tags every single day like a countdown.

When I wake up, it's dark outside, and Colt is still here, still solid, still real. His arms are around me, and I can feel his breath against my hair, and for the first time in six months, I feel like I can breathe properly.

"You're still here," I whisper.

"Told you. As long as you'll let me stay."

"How is this going to work? You're in California. I'm here. The program says eighteen more months—"

"We'll figure it out." His arms tighten. "I'm very good at solving problems. And this? This is a problem worth solving."

I turn in his arms to face him. "CJ is going to kill you if he finds out."

"CJ knows."

I blink. "What?"

"He gave me your location. After the psych eval. After I passed all his tests." Colt stops and takes in a deep breath, looks at me like I'm his entire world. "He said some people are worth breaking the rules for. That I should stop punishing myself and go get what I want."

Tears blur my vision. "CJ is a romantic."

"CJ is a strategic pain in the ass who wants his best operator back in fighting shape."

"So he told you where I was."

"Something like that."

I touch the dog tags around my neck. "You're really here. For me. Even though it's complicated and messy and—"

"Yeah, Magnolia. I'm really here." He pulls me closer. "Because six months ago, I made you a promise. Two years, I said. But I'm realizing now that was bullshit. I was always going to come. Whether it was six months or six days. I was always going to find you."

"Why?"

"Because you made me feel something real. First time in five years. Because you're strong, fierce. Because—" He stops, swallows. "Because choosing you feels like choosing right for once. And I'm done choosing wrong."

The tears come again, but this time they're good tears. Relief tears. Six months of holding myself together finally allowed to crack apart because someone's here to catch the pieces.

"Stay," I tell him. "However long you can. Just—stay."

"Okay."

"And then come back. When you have to leave. Come back."

"Okay."

"And in eighteen months when this is over—"

"I'll be right here. Waiting. Ready." His hand cups my face.

"Whatever comes next, we figure it out together. No more counting down days alone. No more pretending we can wait when we can't. We do this together."

Together.

The word settles into my chest like a promise.

Like a choice.

Like the beginning of something that started in violence and fear, but might turn into something good.

Something real.

Something worth fighting for.

"Together," I agree.

And when he kisses me this time, it feels like a beginning.

Not an ending.

Not a pause.

A beginning.

Of Colt and Maggie. Frost and Magnolia. Two people who chose each other when choosing was dangerous and maybe a little bit crazy.

But some choices are worth making anyway.

Some promises are worth keeping even when they break the rules.

And some people—some people — are worth crossing state lines, violating witness protection protocols, and showing up six months early because waiting feels impossible.

Colt Harrison is one of those people.

And I'm going to choose him right back.

Again and again and again.

For however long this lasts.

For whatever comes next.

Together.

My phone buzzes with CJ's name flashing on the screen. I show it to Colt.

"Fuck." He pulls at his chin. "Shouldn't be surprised."

"Do I answer?"

"If you don't, he'll just hound you."

I answer on the sixth ring. "Hello?"

"Maggie," CJ says, voice gravelly but warm, the kind of tone that brooks no bullshit but carries respect. "I've got a job if you're interested. Guardian HRS is thinking about standing up a new team. Guardian Angels. All-female unit. We need someone with your... unique experience to help stand it up."

"Excuse me?"

"It will take a minimum of eighteen months to reach full operational capacity. You'll relocate to Guardian HQ, live on base the whole time. Probably won't be able to leave until the unit's operational."

I laugh, a real one, sharp and relieved, seeing right through the offer. He's not recruiting; he's engineering this—tying my future to Colt's orbit without forcing it, giving us space to build while locking down the threats that still whisper in the dark.

"You're a meddler, CJ."

"Strategic planner," he corrects, but I hear the smile in his voice. "Frost's been useless for six months. Figured I'd solve two problems at once. You in?"

I look at Colt, who's watching me with an expression I'm starting to recognize. Not love—not yet. But the foundation of it. The possibility of it.

"Yeah," I say, grinning into the empty room, the weight lifting like dawn breaking. "I'm in."

The call ends and I stare at my phone.

"Guardian Angels," Colt says. "CJ's been planning that for years. All-female tactical unit for ops where male operators would compromise the mission."

"Hostage rescue in conservative countries?" I see it.

"Undercover work in trafficking rings."

"Close protection for female VIPs."

"Yeah." He pulls me back down beside him. "CJ's smart. He saw what you did at that ranch. Former Army medic who can shoot, move, and communicate under fire. You're exactly what he needs."

"What about what I need."

His arm tightens around me. "Eighteen months on base. With me. Building something good. That work for you?"

"Yeah, that works." I touch the dog tags. Sofia's ghost is finally released.

AUTHOR'S NOTE:
Thank you for reading FROST!

IF YOU'RE CRAVING MORE HIGH-STAKES MISSIONS, MORALLY GRAY operators, and romance forged in gunfire—I've got you covered.

BINGE THE GUARDIAN HOSTAGE RESCUE SPECIALISTS (HRS) WORLD NOW

THE GUARDIAN HRS UNIVERSE IS MASSIVE, AND MULTIPLE complete series are waiting for you:

🔥 **GUARDIAN HRS CORE SERIES** - *COMPLETE AND READY to binge* **Alpha, Bravo, Charlie,** and **Delta** teams handling the extractions governments won't touch. These operators live in the shadows, fight in the dark, and fall hard for the women who make them want to step into the light.
- Elite hostage rescue specialists
- International black ops missions
- Brothers-in-arms who become family
- The women tough enough to love them

START WITH ALPHA TEAM, BOOK 1 → RESCUING ZOE → READ HERE

CERBERUS PERSONAL SECURITY SERIES -*GHOST*, ***BRASS***, and **Whisper,** *with more coming soon.*

THE **CERBERUS** SERIES IS GUARDIAN HRS ADJACENT - **Grittier, Darker, More Possessive**

When Guardian HRS needs someone protected but the threat level is DEFCON 1, they call Cerberus. These aren't your typical bodyguards—they're the operators who live between protection and elimination. More alpha. More possessive. More willing to cross lines the Guardians won't.

Think: Dominant protector heroes who'll burn the world down to keep their woman safe.

- Close protection with deadly force authorized
- Operators who don't play by the rules
- Obsessive, possessive, "mine to protect" romance
- Higher heat, darker themes

START WITH **GHOST** → READ HERE

CAN'T DECIDE? WANT IT ALL?

→ Read Guardian HRS first (it's the foundation), then dive into Cerberus for the grittier adjacent operations.

THE GUARDIAN HRS PROMISE:

Every book features:

- ☑ Competent, dangerous heroes with hidden depths
- ☑ Strong heroines who don't need saving (but get protected anyway)

☑ Found family and brotherhood
☑ Realistic tactical operations (I do my research)
☑ Romance that earns the HEA
☑ Standalone books with interconnected world

DON'T WAIT - START YOUR BINGE NOW

A PERSONAL INVITATION

Colt and Maggie's story is a 25,000 word **NOVELLA**—just a taste and a quick, intense introduction to the Guardian HRS world. But here's what you need to know: **nearly every other book in this universe is a massive, extra-long novel.**

We're talking 80,000-100,000+ words of:
- Complex multi-layered missions
- Deep character development
- Multiple POVs and subplots
- Extended tactical operations
- Slow-burn romance that EARNS the payoff
- Brotherhood dynamics and found family

FROST gave you a taste. The full series gives you a FEAST.

Think of this novella as your amuse-bouche—a carefully crafted bite designed to show you what I'm capable of.

. . .

THE MAIN GUARDIAN HRS AND CERBERUS BOOKS? THOSE ARE five-course meals. Beefy, satisfying, the kind of novels you lose an entire weekend to because you physically cannot put them down.

IF COLT AND MAGGIE'S STORY RESONATED WITH YOU IN JUST 25,000 words—if you felt Colt's guilt, Maggie's betrayal, and the desperate need for something REAL in a world of lies—imagine what I can do with **four times the page count.**

THE FULL-LENGTH NOVELS DIVE DEEP:
- Operators with complex trauma and layered backstories
- Missions that span multiple countries and weeks of operations
- Romance that develops over hundreds of pages (not hours)
- Secondary characters who become your new obsessions
- Plot twists that will make you gasp at 2 AM
- Action sequences that feel like watching a movie

The Guardian HRS world is waiting.
Your next operator is loading his weapon.
And you've got 30+ extra-long novels ready to devour.

WHICH TEAM WILL YOU CHOOSE?

STAY DANGEROUS,

Ellie Masters

🔥 START BINGING NOW 🔥

Guardian HRS Alpha Team, Book 1: RESCUING ZOE →
CLICK HERE

Cerberus Book 1: GHOST → CLICK HERE

The Guardian HRS world has **30+** complete books waiting for you. Operators are falling in love. Missions are launching. And somewhere in this universe, your next *book boyfriend* is loading his weapon and preparing to risk everything for the woman who makes him feel human again.

🎯 READY FOR YOUR NEXT MISSION?

ELLZ BELLZ

ELLIE'S FACEBOOK READER GROUP

If you are interested in joining the **ELLZ BELLZ**, Ellie's Facebook reader group, we'd love to have you.

Join Ellie's **ELLZ BELLZ**.
The **ELLZ BELLZ** Facebook Reader Group

Sign up for Ellie's Newsletter.
Elliemasters.com/newslettersignup

START HERE

Rockstar Romance

The Angel Fire Rock Romance Series

EACH BOOK IN THIS SERIES CAN BE READ AS A STANDALONE AND IS ABOUT A DIFFERENT COUPLE WITH AN HEA.

IT IS RECOMMENDED THEY ARE READ IN ORDER.

Heart's Insanity

Ashes to New

Heart's Desire

Heart's Collide

Hearts Divided

Hearts Entwined

Forest's FALL

Hearts The Last Beat

CONTINUE HERE...

Military Romance

Guardian Hostage Rescue Specialists

Rescuing Melissa

(Get a FREE copy of Rescuing Melissa

when you join Ellie's Newsletter)

Alpha Team

Rescuing Zoe

Rescuing Moira

Rescuing Eve

Rescuing Lily

Rescuing Jinx

Rescuing Maria

Bravo Team

Rescuing Angie

Rescuing Isabelle

Rescuing Carmen

Rescuing Rosalie

Rescuing Kaye

Cara's Protector

Rescuing Barbi

Charlie Team

Rescuing Rebel

Rescuing Stitch

Rescuing Mia

Jenna's Protector

Rescuing Sophia

Rescuing Malia

Rescuing Ally (Part 1)

Rescuing Ally (Part 2)

Delta Team

Rescuing Ember

Rescuing Aria

STANDALONES IN THE GUARDIAN HOSTAGE RESCUE SERIES YOU CAN READ ANYTIME

Military Romance

Guardian Personal Protection Specialists

Sybil's Protector

Lyra's Protector

Angel's Peak Series

Steamy Instalove Small Town

Snowed in with the Mountain Doctor

Rescued by the Mountain Guide

Stranded with the Resort Owner

Matched with the Small-Town Chef

Trapped with the Forest Ranger

Snowbound with the Vineyard Owner

Reunited with the Hometown Hero

Colliding with the Coffee Shop Owner

Falling for the Firefighter

Wrecked with the Reclusive Author

Tangled with the Single Dad

Whirlwinded by the Helicopter Pilot

Sheltered by the Veterinarian

Bound by the Sheriff

The One I Want Series
(Small Town, Military Heroes)
By Jet & Ellie Masters

Saving Abby

Saving Ariel

Saving Brie

Saving Cate

Saving Dani

Saving Jen

The LaRouge Triplets

Asher

Brody

Cage

Billionaire Romance

Billionaire Boys Club

Hawke

Richard

Contemporary Romance

Cocky Captain

Romantic Suspense

EACH BOOK IS A STANDALONE NOVEL.

The Starling

The Swan

~AND~

Science Fiction

Ellie Masters writing as L.A. Warren
Vendel Rising: a Science Fiction Serialized Novel

If you enjoyed this book by Ellie Masters, the LIGHTER SIDE of the Jet & Ellie writing duo, and aren't afraid of edgier writing, you might enjoy reading BDSM themed books written by Jet, the DARKER SIDE of the Masters' Writing Team.

The DARKER SIDE

Jet Masters is the darker side of the Jet & Ellie writing duo!

Romantic Suspense

Changing Roles Series:

THIS SERIES MUST BE READ IN ORDER.

Command Me

Control Me

Collar Me

Embracing FATE

Seizing FATE

Accepting FATE

HOT READS

A STANDALONE NOVEL.

Down the Rabbit Hole

Light BDSM Romance

The Ties that Bind

EACH BOOK IN THIS SERIES CAN BE READ AS A STANDALONE AND IS ABOUT A DIFFERENT COUPLE WITH AN HEA.

Alexa

Penny

Michelle

Ivy

HOT READS

Becoming His Series

THIS SERIES MUST BE READ IN ORDER.

The Ballet

Learning to Breathe

Becoming His

Dark Captive Romance

A STANDALONE NOVEL.

She's MINE

About the Author

Ellie Masters is a USA Today Bestselling author and Amazon Top 15 Author who writes Angsty, Steamy, Heart-Stopping, Pulse-Pounding, Can't-Stop-Reading Romantic Suspense. In addition, she's a wife, military mom, doctor, and retired Colonel. She writes romantic suspense filled with all your sexy, swoon-worthy alpha men. Her writing will tug at your heartstrings and leave your heart racing.

Born in the South, raised under the Hawaiian sun, Ellie has traveled the globe while in service to her country. The love of her life, her amazing husband, is her number one fan and biggest supporter. And yes! He's read every word she's written.

She has lived all over the United States—east, west, north, south and central—but grew up under the Hawaiian sun. She's also been privileged to have lived overseas, experiencing other cultures and making lifelong friends. Now, Ellie is proud to call herself a Southern transplant, learning to say y'all and "bless her heart" with the best of them.

Ellie's favorite way to spend an evening is curled up on a couch, laptop in place, watching a fire, drinking a good wine, and bringing forth all the characters from her mind to the page and hopefully into the hearts of her readers.

FOR MORE INFORMATION
elliemasters.com

Connect with Ellie Masters

Website:
elliemasters.com
Purchase Direct:
elliemasters.com/shopify
Amazon Author Page:
elliemasters.com/amazon
Facebook:
elliemasters.com/Facebook
Goodreads:
elliemasters.com/Goodreads
Bookbub:
elliemasters.com/Bookbub
Instagram:
elliemasters.com/Instagram

Final Thoughts

I hope you enjoyed this book as much as I enjoyed writing it. If you enjoyed reading this story, please consider leaving a review on Amazon and Goodreads, and please let other people know. A sentence is all it takes. Friend recommendations are the strongest catalyst for readers' purchase decisions! And I'd love to be able to continue bringing the characters and stories from My-Mind-to-the-Page.

Second, call or e-mail a friend and tell them about this book. If you really want them to read it, gift it to them. If you prefer digital friends, please use the "Recommend" feature of Goodreads to spread the word.

Or visit my blog https://elliemasters.com, where you can find out more about my writing process and personal life.

Come visit The EDGE: Dark Discussions where we'll have a chance to talk about my works, their creation, and maybe what the future has in store for my writing.

Facebook Reader Group: Ellz Bellz

Thank you so much for your support!

Love,

Ellie

Dedication

This book is dedicated to you, my reader. Thank you for spending a few hours of your time with me. I wouldn't be able to write without you to cheer me on. Your wonderful words, your support, and your willingness to join me on this journey is a gift beyond measure.

Whether this is the first book of mine you've read, or if you've been with me since the very beginning, thank you for believing in me as I bring these characters 'from my mind to the page and into your hearts.'

Love,
Ellie

THE END